RAVE REVIEWS FOR
FRANCIS RAY

NOBODY BUT YOU

"A story that tugs at the heartstrings."
—*Romantic Times BOOKreviews*

"Fast and fun and full of emotional thrills and sexy chills. Everything a racing romance should be!"
—Roxanne St. Claire

"Not only does Francis Ray rock in this book but you also see a whole different side of racing that will keep you on the edge of your seat." —*Night Owl Romance*

"A wonderful read." —*Fresh Fiction*

UNTIL THERE WAS YOU

"Ms. Ray has given us a great novel again. Did we expect anything less than the best?"
—*Romantic Times BOOKreviews* (4 stars)

"Crisp style, realistic dialogue, likable characters, and [a] fast pace." —*Library Journal*

THE WAY YOU LOVE ME

"A romance that will have readers speed-reading to the next tension-filled scene, if not the climax."
—*Fresh Fiction*

"Fans of Ray's Grayson and Falcon families will be thrilled with the first installment in the new Grayson Friends series. And this is done very well . . . told with such grace and affection that this novel is a treat to read." —*Romantic Times BOOKreviews* (4 stars)

"Francis Ray is, without a doubt, one of the Queens of Romance." —*A Romance Review*

ONLY YOU

"Francis Ray's graceful writing style and realistically complex characters give her latest contemporary romance its extraordinary emotional richness and depth."

—*Chicago Tribune*

"It's a joy to read this always fresh and exciting saga." —*Romantic Times BOOKreviews* (4 stars)

"The powerful descriptive powers of Francis Ray allow the reader to step into the story and become an active part of the surrender . . . If you love a great love story, *Only You* should be on your list."

—*Fallen Angel Reviews*

"Riveting emotion and charismatic scenes that made this book captivating . . . a beautiful story of love and romance." —*Night Owl Romance*

"A beautiful love story as only Francis Ray can tell it."
—Singletitles.com

"Readers will find a warm and wonderful contemporary romance with plenty of humor and drama. Adding a fun warmth and reality to these characters and a plot that moves quickly add all the needed incentive to read this fun book." —*Multicultural Romance Writers*

IRRESISTIBLE YOU

"A pleasurable story . . . a well-developed story and continuous plot." —*Romantic Times BOOKreviews*

"Like the previous titles in this series, *Irresistible You* is another winner . . . Witty and charming . . . Author Francis Ray has a true gift for drawing the readers in and never letting them go."
—*Multicultural Romance Writers*

DREAMING OF YOU

"A great read from beginning to end, it's even excellent for an immediate re-read."
—*Romantic Times BOOKreviews*

"An immensely likable heroine, a sexy man with a heart of gold, and touches of glitz and color, [this] is as unapologetically escapist as Cinderella. Lots of fun."
—*BookPage*

YOU AND NO OTHER

"The warmth and sincerity of the Graysons bring another book to life . . . delightfully realistic."
—*Romantic Times*

"Astonishing sequel . . . the best romance of the new year . . . the Graysons are sure to leave a smile on your face and a longing in your heart for their next story."
—*ARomanceReview.com*

"There are three more [Grayson] children with great love stories in the future." —*Booklist*

SOMEONE TO LOVE ME

"Another great romance novel." —*Booklist*

"The plot moves quickly, and the characters are interesting." —*Romantic Times*

"The characters give as good as they get, and their romance is very believable." —*All About Romance*

BREAK EVERY RULE

"Francis Ray is a literary chanteuse, crooning the most sensual romantic fiction melodies in a compelling performance of skill and talent that culminates in another solid gold hit!"
—Romantic Times

HEART OF THE FALCON

"[A] well-written, tender story about a man growing into respect and trust."
—Publishers Weekly

"A new romance you won't want to miss with characters that are so real, you get involved in their lives. Splendid romance by Francis Ray! *Heart of the Falcon* is superb!"
—Literary Times

"Ray has created another sure-to-be bestseller sizzler that will singe your mind with the laughter, tenderness, and passion that smolders between the pages."
—Romantic Times

A Dangerous Kiss

FRANCIS RAY

St. Martin's Paperbacks

This is a work of fiction. All of the characters, organizations, and events portrayed in this novel are either products of the author's imagination or are used fictitiously.

A DANGEROUS KISS

For information address St. Martin's Press, 175 Fifth Avenue, New York, NY 10010.

ISBN: 978-0-312-53649-7

Printed in the United States of America

St. Martin's Paperbacks edition / July 2012

St. Martin's Paperbacks are published by St. Martin's Press, 175 Fifth Avenue, New York, NY 10010.

10 9 8 7 6 5 4 3

Chapter 1

Payton "Sin" Sinclair was an unapologetic people-watcher. As a sports consultant, working with some of the biggest and most recognizable athletes in sports and business, he had to be able to read the smallest nuances of others. That ability was just one of the unique attributes that set him apart from the competition and made him the go-to person when corporations wanted to align themselves with the top professional athletes in the country.

On a beautiful Sunday afternoon, Sin was sipping a nice vintage wine and helping celebrate the recently announced engagement of C. J. Callahan, one of his two best friends, in the lavish East Hampton home of C. J.'s elated parents. Just because Sin was standing with C. J. and Alex Stewart, Sin's other best friend, and enjoying himself didn't mean he'd stopped noticing the people around him, especially those he cared deeply about.

Since he'd long ago developed the ability to listen with one ear while observing—it was critical at sports games, with so much going on—Sin listened to C. J. go on and on about what a great woman Cicely was and how lucky he was, while Sin watched Summer Radcliffe chat with a beaming Cicely St. John, C. J.'s fiancée, in the elegant, French-inspired great room.

The other woman with them was Dianne Harrington Stewart, the new wife of Alex. Dianne, a stunning long-legged former international fashion model, looked as happy as Cicely. On the other hand, Summer's usual smile and vibrancy were noticeably missing . . . at least to him.

He'd first noticed Summer's pensiveness when Dianne and Alex were dating and had an argument outside C. J.'s bar, Callahan's. Summer had completely stunned Sin by musing that, when Dianne and Alex settled their disagreement and kissed, they would later have makeup sex.

Sin couldn't get her startling comment out of his mind. It bothered him that he hadn't been able to tell if she'd been wistful or frustrated. Not once in their long friendship had he ever heard her mention sex. Truthfully, it stunned him a bit that she had. She wasn't the type of woman to take intimacy lightly or talk about it openly. Afterward, she'd ignored his attempts to find out if the comment had been offhand or something more, and had gone inside the bar to play pool with Dianne.

Sin traveled a great deal, but he hadn't heard about Summer being in a relationship. Her cousin C. J. was as protective of Summer as he was of his younger sister, Ariel. After Summer's parents' death, she had gone to live with her mother's only sibling, C. J.'s mother.

C. J. certainly would have mentioned it if Summer was serious about a man . . . if he had known. Lately C. J. had a full plate with Callahan Software, Callahan's Bar, and Cicely. It disturbed Sin that some idiot might have slipped past C. J. Worse, that the idiot didn't appreciate what a wonderful woman he had. Sin's eyes narrowed dangerously. If he found out that was the case, he would take care of it himself. No one, absolutely no one, took advantage of Summer while he breathed.

From the moment they met when she was just out of high school and dealing with the death of her parents, he'd felt protective of her. Despite her tragic loss, she'd worked her butt off to make her parents' dream of owning a successful upscale restaurant in Manhattan a reality. He admired her determination, loyalty, and tenacity.

She hadn't had it easy in life. Perhaps because he'd lost his father when he was eighteen, and she'd lost her parents at the same age, he felt a certain empathy and closeness with her. If at all possible, he was going to figure out what was bothering her and fix it. He didn't like seeing a forced smile on her beautiful face.

At least he knew her pensiveness wasn't due to the unfortunate incident that could have damaged the reputation of Radcliffe's. It still angered the hell out of him that a woman he'd rebuffed had tried to get back at him by spreading vicious rumors about Summer's restaurant. The spiteful socialite had seen him in the newspaper with his arm around Summer while she was catering at his suite at Yankee Stadium and drawn the wrong conclusion. Once he'd learned of the woman's lies, he'd confronted her at a high-profile social function and warned her to admit the lies or suffer the consequences.

She'd caved and became the one gossiped about. For a while Summer hadn't been too pleased with him, blaming the incident on him dating so many women. It had taken weeks for her to fully forgive him and for their easy camaraderie to return. He'd do anything for them never to be at odds again.

A broad hand clasped Sin on the shoulder, breaking into his thoughts. He looked up into C. J.'s handsome, clean-shaven face, which had always made him extremely popular with the women. "Thanks for being my best man."

With his dark eyes twinkling in his bearded face, Sin tipped his wineglass toward C. J. Both men were over six feet, but while C. J. had the broad shoulders of a linebacker, Sin was lean and muscular. "Thank me when I drag you away from the blowout bachelor party Alex and I are going to give you so you can be at your best for your wedding."

C. J.'s laughter was pure wickedness. "I might leave before then. I can't wait for Cicely to be completely mine. She gave up her dream for me."

The words were barely out of his mouth when his attention shifted to where the women were standing. Sin could tell by the rapt expression on C. J.'s face that he and Cicely had gotten lost in each other's gaze again, as they had off and on since their arrival two hours ago. For them, everyone else in the elegantly decorated room had ceased to exist.

"I think we lost him," Alex said with a burst of laughter. "Again."

Alex—a successful Manhattan lawyer with a Who's Who list of clients, as well as the people no one ever heard of but whose cases he took because he hated to see people screwed over—stood at a trim six foot two. Like Sin, Alex liked to dress well. Today he was comfortably dressed in chocolate slacks and a tan linen short-sleeved shirt. C. J., who favored jeans and T-shirts if he wasn't in corporate mode running the family-owned Callahan Software company, wore navy dress slacks and a white shirt in honor of the special occasion.

"I seem to recall you being the same way," Sin reminded Alex. When Dianne wasn't working at her and Alex's fashion design house, D&A of New York, or Alex wasn't at work, they were usually together. Placing his champagne flute on the tray of a nearby waiter, Sin caught C. J.'s arm. "Let's put him out of his misery."

"Let's." Alex caught C. J.'s other arm, and they led him to his waiting fiancée.

They were barely there when C. J. reached out and tenderly pulled Cicely into his arms and kissed her. Always fashionable, she wore a sunny yellow dress that bared smooth shoulders and stopped inches above a pair of great-looking knees. Elegant, sophisticated, and gorgeous—it was easy to see why Cicely was the fashion director at one of the most influential high-fashion magazines in the country.

"Happy?" C. J. asked.

"I've never been happier." Cicely leaned into the shelter of C. J.'s six-foot-four frame, her head against his broad chest.

"I plan to keep you that way." C. J. gave her another kiss.

Dianne, in a short sleeveless magenta dress that showed off her famous legs, walked into her husband's open arms. While the newly engaged snuggled and the newly married looked on approvingly and did the same thing, Sin watched Summer. There was a smile on her striking face that was serene and restful, but there was also a hint of sadness in her dark chocolate eyes. The sparkle of happiness and teasing warmth that had unknowingly gotten him through a couple of rough days in the last four months wasn't there.

Sin didn't think; he just stepped forward and curved his arm around Summer's slim waist. Her arm went around him without hesitation. They'd done this a thousand times, but he'd never felt as he did now—that there was a barrier between them he couldn't break through to comfort her. He didn't like the feeling. At the moment, there were too many things in his personal life that were out of his control. He didn't want to add another.

Sin felt the slight trembling of Summer's slim body, and pulled her just the tiniest bit closer as he glanced down at her.

He saw what she undoubtedly wanted everyone to see, a beautifully poised and stylish woman in a white sheath that accentuated her shapely, slim five-foot-five body to perfection. The coal-black wavy hair that usually hung free and reached to the middle of her back was in some kind of intricate twist on top of her head. The upsweep made her slender neck appear vulnerable, her heart-shaped face more alluring. Any man would be proud to call her his.

"Looks like we're the odd ones out," Sin said, trying to tease her into smiling for real.

"Yes," she said without looking at him.

Sin wondered if anyone else heard the tiniest tremble in her voice. He'd take her for a walk on the beach behind the estate as they'd done so many times after she'd lost her parents and in the years since, if he thought he'd get an answer. He wouldn't. Summer could be as tight-lipped as the clams she served in Radcliffe's, her five-star restaurant in Upper Manhattan.

"I don't supposed you've changed your minds about having the engagement party at Callahan's and letting your father and me book a more appropriate place or have it here," C. J.'s mother, Evelyn, asked hopefully.

"Nope." C. J. curved his free arm around his mother's tense shoulders. "My bar it is."

"I suppose Summer will cater," his mother said, lines forming in her otherwise smooth forehead. "I realize you, Cicely, and Summer don't need help with the menu, but you know I'm here if you need me."

Cicely and C. J. shared a resigned look, then Cicely said, "Mrs. Callahan, about the menu. We've decided to have hamburgers and onion rings. It's the first meal I ate at Callahan's."

Mrs. Callahan's eyes widened with horror. C. J. plucked a glass from a nearby waiter and handed it to her. She lifted the flute to her mouth without hesitation.

"The crew at the bar wanted to do it for us," C. J. explained as his mother took another sip. "We hope you and Dad will understand."

"Of course, son," his father said, an indulgent smile on his handsome face.

He and C. J.'s older brother, Paul, had suffered some serious health issues in the past, so C. J. was running Callahan Software and had a manager running his baby, Callahan's Bar. Thank goodness both C. J.'s father and his brother were doing well.

"It is *your* wedding," C. J.'s father continued.

Mrs. Callahan lowered the glass and frowned up

at her husband. He smiled and took the almost empty glass from her. "Isn't that right, Evelyn?"

"Of course . . . It's just I wanted something a bit more lavish for you."

Sin knew the bride-to-be's parents usually threw the engagement party, but that wasn't likely to happen. When C. J.'s brother and his wife had their engagement announcement party, both sets of parents worked together to have the affair at the Waldorf for more than two hundred intimate family members and friends. It had been spectacular and a night to remember.

"We understand," C. J. said, smiling into his mother's troubled face. "That's why besides helping plan the wedding, we're giving you carte blanche on planning the rehearsal dinner."

Mrs. Callahan's eyes brightened with pleasure. "Really?"

"Please," Cicely said, placing her hand on her future mother-in-law's shoulder. "Regardless of what your son thinks, we both know that eleven months—"

"I wanted the wedding in six weeks," C. J. interrupted.

"—is not enough time to plan the type of formal wedding we're having," Cicely continued as if C. J. hadn't spoken. "With C. J.'s and my busy schedule, which frequently takes us both out of town, you planning the last time we'll see each other before we become husband and wife will mean so much to both of us."

Mrs. Callahan hugged Cicely and then C. J. "It will be fabulous and memorable. I promise."

"We know." C. J. smiled at his mother. "And I promise we won't get too rowdy and embarrass you and the family at the engagement party."

"You could never do that." C. J.'s father said. "We're proud of you, son, and proud of Cicely. Even if the women will now outnumber the men. We might never get to watch another sports game on television."

C. J. playfully winked at his father. "I'm turning Cicely into a sports fan. She'll be on our side."

Cicely's smile was all teeth. "I might enjoy sports, but I can think for myself. It would behoove you not to forget it."

C. J. threw back his head and let out a shout of laughter. "Is it any wonder I love you? You'll never let me get the big head."

"And you'll never let me forget how much I'm loved," Cicely said, her voice the barest whisper of sound.

"Always," C. J. said, his voice sure and strong.

C. J.'s mother sniffed, dabbed her eyes with a fresh tissue her husband handed her. Sin noticed that she'd gone through several. Clearly C. J.'s parents were enormously happy for him and Cicely, but her parents had declined the invitation from C. J.'s parents to the Sunday brunch, saying they didn't have "enough time" to make flight arrangements from Columbia, South Carolina. C. J. told Sin that her parents had said the same thing when Cicely called. Sin had offered to send his private jet for them, but they'd politely declined as well.

Family could be a blessing or a curse. No one knew that better than Sin.

Stepping away from Sin, Summer plucked a flute from a nearby waiter's tray. "I'd like to propose a toast to my cousin C. J., and his fiancée and my friend Cicely." Summer kept her flute raised as C. J.'s sister, his brother, and his wife joined them. "To C. J. and Cicely, wishing you every happiness on your journey of forever together. May each day bring your closer, make your love stronger."

"To C. J. and Cicely," people chorused as the distinct click of crystal flutes sounded.

Sin drank his wine, but he never took his gaze from Summer. Her hand was steady, the sparkle finally back in her incredible eyes. Whatever it was had passed. While he was glad, he intended to find out what had put the sadness in her lovely face.

Sin was watching her.

In the past, the knowledge that he was always there had given Summer a certain amount of comfort. At the moment, it made her want to squirm and hang her head. And, unlike in the past, he was the last person she could talk to about the reason. At least the party was over.

Bidding her family and Cicely good-bye, Summer climbed inside the limousine Sin had hired to drive him, Alex, Dianne, and her up to the Hamptons from New York. He had a vintage Aston Martin convertible two-seater, but he seldom drove it, preferring a car service.

Scooting over, Summer kept the practiced smile on her face. She'd considered leaving early, could even think of so many plausible excuses that she could have used. Sin would have insisted the driver take her back to town. But that would be the coward's way. She wouldn't add that to her shame.

What was the matter with her that she couldn't move past this . . . this feeling that kept circling her and coming back to nip her on the backside no matter how much she fought it?

How could this have happened to her? It made no sense, but that didn't change it or make it go away.

It had just snuck up on her when she hadn't been looking or expecting it. Sin was one of her best friends. He wasn't supposed to make her skin tingle, her body have the strong desire to lean closer, to brush her lips across his, to feel the softness of his beard against her cheek.

And no matter how hard she tried to stop the new feelings, they wouldn't go away. She suspected they had started when, a couple of months ago, she'd begun to catch glimpses of sadness in his expression, which before had always been filled with laughter and teasing. She hadn't asked about the reason because the occasions were so fleeting.

Or was it because she hadn't wanted to hear that it had been because of a woman?

Summer blew out a breath and waited for the rest to get inside the limo. Perhaps that was why she'd caught herself teasing him about the women in his life: She'd been hoping to gain information. She never did. Sin wasn't the type of man to talk about his women. But she had no doubt they were many. He and C. J. both had reputations for women going in and out of their lives like revolving doors, but once out, they were never invited back.

If that wasn't enough for her to deal with, the Li'l Green Monster had decided to perch on her shoulder.

She'd felt horrible that she hadn't been able to shake the feeling that men she thought were confirmed bachelors had somehow found the loves of their lives while she was still searching. That Summer now called the women they'd found friends somehow made the ache worse.

Alex and Dianne might have known each other since they were children, but C. J. and Cicely hadn't. Yet, somehow, they'd managed to find each other and fall in love.

Everyone around her seemed to be having a summer romance, heading to the altar, or having a baby while Summer remained alone. She wasn't lonely. She was too busy for that, but she wished there was one special person—someone attainable—to share the day with, to talk about nothing, or just to hold and watch the sun set.

Still, she had no right to feel the twinge of jealousy. She had so much to be thankful for. She was living her dream, running Radcliffe's. Hundreds of restaurants opened and promptly closed in New York while Radcliffe's thrived. Her envy made her feel like an ogre. She didn't like the feeling and planned to do something about it. Sin might be giving her some bad moments, but he had also helped her to see that not facing her problems head-on only made the situation worse.

Summer accepted that the only time she had become truly angry with Sin had been due to jealousy. At the time she hadn't thought so. It occurred the night a customer told Summer that an acquaintance claimed that, besides horrible food and slow service at Radcliffe's, she'd seen a rat on her way to the ladies' room. The socialite had warned all of her friends not to patronize the restaurant. Since the customer had never encountered a problem of any sort at the restaurant, she hadn't listened, but she'd wanted Summer to know about the claim.

It had taken all of Summer's professionalism and training not to show her anger, just thank the customer for her continued patronage and calmly refute the other woman's accusations. She'd personally seated the customer and promised to check back from time to time. Two hours later, the customer and her party had left with smiles and accolades for the food and service.

Sin had been dining that night with two of his

clients. She'd told him as soon as the opportunity presented itself. To her surprise, he knew the socialite and the reason she had targeted Radcliffe's. Summer had never seen him so angry, but she had been just as angry that the woman had tried to ruin her restaurant to get back at Sin. Unjustly, Summer had blamed Sin for the woman's lies. It had taken her weeks to get over her annoyance at him, annoyance that was probably heightened by her growing attraction to him.

"That was fun," Dianne said as she slid in on the other side of the limo. Alex climbed in beside her. "Reminds me of our engagement party."

Alex kissed her on the cheek. "The second happiest day of my life. The happiest was when we were married."

Sin entered the car in time to hear Alex's comment. Thankfully, he left a good two feet between him and Summer. "Cut it out, you two."

Dianne grinned, leaned against her husband, and crossed her long legs. "One day you and Summer will feel the same way about someone."

"Not if I can help it," Sin said, then turned to Summer. "How about you?"

Summer's smile slipped a notch. Of all the men for her body to lust after, Sin was the absolute worst. Why settle for one peach when you had the orchard? "I'm too busy," she managed, then, "Oh, I forgot my purse,"

Sin placed his hand on hers when she started to get up. "I'll get it. Where did you leave it?"

She shouldn't be feeling the tingling sensation that radiated up her arm, the arousing heat. He'd touched her thousands of times over the years. "Not sure. I'll be back." Climbing out her side, she hurried up the walk and into the house.

Luckily, the two people she sought were in the first of the three foyers, wrapped in each other's arms kissing. The rest of the family was nowhere in sight. Apparently they understood that C. J. and Cicely wanted to be alone. Summer picked up her envelope purse from behind the vase, exactly where she had intentionally left it. "Excuse me."

C. J. slowly lifted his head. Cicely straightened. "I thought you were gone," he said.

"I came back for this." Summer lifted the purse and took a deep breath. "You guys know I love you, right?"

Cicely immediately pulled free of C. J. and came to her, placing her slim hand on her shoulder. "Of course. What is it?"

C. J. frowned. "You all right?"

Summer nodded. "I don't know how to say it except straight out. A couple of times this afternoon, just for a moment or two, I was jealous. Looking at Alex and Dianne, and now you two bursting with happiness, I'm beginning to feel as if my time will never come."

They both hugged her at once. Cicely spoke first. "I've had more than a few jealous moments in my life. It was difficult enough admitting it to myself. I never had the courage to admit it to anyone else."

"I was jealous of Sin because he and Cicely got along so well and I couldn't think of a thing to say to her," C. J. admitted. "I'd rather eat brussels sprouts than admit it to him."

Summer might not be lucky in love, but she was with friends and relatives. Not only had C. J. and Cicely accepted her apology, they'd commended her. "I'm glad you found each other," Summer said, the tension gone from her body.

Cicely leaned against C. J. "I wasn't expecting C. J. I had my life all planned."

"Speaking of plans, don't forget you asked to meet me and Dianne a week from Wednesday night at six at Radcliffe's," Summer reminded her, sure she was going to be asked to be a bridesmaid for the tenth time.

"Thank you. I know you're busy. I didn't want to take you away from the restaurant so soon after today or I would have invited you to my place," Cicely explained.

Summer smiled to reassure her. "I'm looking forward to girl talk and no testosterone."

"I'm meeting her there." C. J. grinned.

"Why am I not surprised." Summer smiled, glad it was real.

"Your day is coming, Summer," Cicely said. "You're beautiful, successful, and intelligent. Love will find you when you least expect it."

"The guy had better be for real, or he and I are going to have a little talk." This time C. J. wasn't smiling.

Summer thought of Sin, fallen-angel handsome and completely off limits. "You don't have to worry. Carry on. See you next Wednesday." Turning, she hurried back outside and saw Sin waiting beside the limo. His dark eyes were narrowed with speculation as he studied her face.

"You aren't the forgetful type." Sin opened the door when she neared.

"C. J.'s never been engaged before." Summer quickly got inside and scooted to the far corner, not daring to look at Sin. She hadn't fooled him, but at least today she wouldn't have to talk about it. He'd bide his time.

Sin, Alex often said, had the tenacity of a pit bull. She might have been able to fool everyone, but not Sin. He'd always seemed to know when something was bothering her.

Since the death of her parents, he'd been there for her. And when C. J. took off to traipse around the world a year after graduating from college, Sin had become even more important in her life. With him, she could be as silent or as angry as she wanted as she worked though the grief of losing her parents so abruptly. They were best buds.

No matter how she might wish otherwise, they could never be anything more.

Chapter 2

Monday morning Sin arrived at his Manhattan office in the Iron Building shortly before eight thirty. He'd already had an hour workout and a two-mile run, before finishing off his morning routine with a three-mile swim at the Athletic Club.

There was a top-notch fitness center in the building of his penthouse, but the Athletic Club was favored by some of the wealthiest men in New York. Membership there had been a good business move, and his savvy accountants had been able to deduct it as such. Sin had made numerous contacts there that had led to lucrative contracts for his clients.

He wasn't stupid enough to go after a particular executive. He was honest enough and smart enough to let the relationships he'd developed over the eight-year membership evolve naturally through a shared love of sports and business savvy. He was honest enough to know his ability to obtain tickets in the front row or a suite for a sold-out sports events had helped.

Placing his black leather briefcase on his sleek

glass-and-metal desk, he turned on the computer and took a seat in the ergonomic chair. After ten years in the business, he had five other offices—Chicago, Austin, Dallas, Phoenix, Charlotte—and the same desk and chair in each, as well as a condo or an apartment. Dallas, his hometown, was the only place besides New York he'd given any thought to making into any type of home.

The computer booted up and he went online to check the sports news as usual. The first image he saw on the twenty-five-inch screen was the angry, bruised face of his client Glen Atkins, an All-Pro running back in the NFL, and a pain in Sin's rear.

A hard frown on his face, Sin reached for the phone on his desk. The call was answered on the third ring.

"Calling this early, I guess you know about Atkins," came the long-suffering voice of Vince Nobles, Atkins's agent.

"What the hell is wrong with Atkins?" Sin barked out the question. "Aren't two paternity suits pending against him enough without being involved in a brawl in a club last night?"

"Now, Sinclair. Glen was just defending himself," Nobles placated. "He didn't throw the first punch."

"If he'd been home as he was told, it would be a moot issue." Sin paced. Lord, deliver him from the ego and sheer stupidity of some professional athletes. A few thought they were above the law and everyone else, grabbing shameful headlines, while the majority of them were hardworking professionals who gave a lot of their time and money to charities. "There's a morality clause in those multimillion-dollar contracts he signed in the past two years. His sponsors could walk."

"I thought you said that smart lawyer friend of yours, Alex Stewart, was the best," Nobles said, his voice finally sounding worried.

"He is. The contract is iron-tight for Glen as well as the corporations. He's the one throwing away his career and life with both hands."

"Glen was just blowing off a bit of steam since the lockout."

Sin cursed under his breath. "I don't see any other NFL players' pictures on the front page of Huffington. I see Glen's. Let him blow off steam in a way that doesn't involve the police and get his name making ugly headlines."

"I'll talk to him."

"You better do more than talk," Sin told the agent. "I placed Atkins with several of his sponsors; my reputation is tied to his."

"Glen is the best in the league. His records of returns and touchdowns can't be touched," Nobles said. "They're lucky to have him."

Sin had heard it too many times over the years. "No one is irreplaceable. Get Atkins to shut it down or be prepared for the fallout. Good-bye."

Sin hung up the phone and finally took his seat.

Ninety-eight percent of the time he loved his job. He'd always enjoyed sports and had lettered in football, basketball, and track. It was a joy matching the best of the best athletes with corporate sponsors.

And the pay wasn't bad, either. A smile worked its way across Sin's bearded face until he glanced at the headline again.

STAR RUNNING BACK IN NIGHTCLUB BRAWL.

"What a waste," Sin muttered. He'd seen it too many times in the past. Too much money and fame too fast had ruined too many careers to count. They didn't learn from the athletes before them. Each one thought he or she was "different." "Irreplaceable." When they learned they weren't, it was too late. Their lives were in shambles, their careers ruined.

Sin had tried to talk to Atkins, but his words of caution had bounced off him like water off a duck's back. That was one person who wouldn't receive an invitation to Sin's first party at his penthouse. Which bought him back to his dilemma—how to get Summer to cater the event.

He was known throughout the sports industry for bringing elite professional sports figures and corporations together. He was also known for doing everything in style. He planned to do just that with an elegant but fun party at his place to thank his clients—which included some of the top athletes and executives in the country.

Leaning back in his chair, Sin linked his fingers behind his dark head and stared out the window across his desk. The affair had to be fantastic in every way, from food and beverages to atmosphere. He wouldn't have to worry about anything if Summer was in charge. She had a unique way with food and presentation and people. Her restaurant, Radcliffe's, had been successful since opening four years ago and had grown from three stars to five.

It was as much a coup as a pleasure for her to occasionally cater at his private suite at Yankee Stadium. His guests always gave her rave reviews, and lamented when she wasn't there. She was definitely a tough act to follow

A frown on his face, he rocked forward. Besides wanting her to cater, he also wanted her to be his hostess. When he'd come up with the idea of the party, she'd been the only woman he'd thought of. With his busy travel schedule, and then C. J.'s engagement, Sin hadn't yet been able to broach the subject with Summer.

He'd planned to ask her at the party yesterday, but he hadn't had a chance. In truth, he'd forgotten about it once he'd seen the unhappiness on her face. As he'd thought, trying to talk to her afterward had been a complete wash, which made Sin even more determined.

He glanced at his thin gold watch, checked his calendar, then set the watch's alarm for 10:00 AM. He'd kill two birds in one fell swoop, visiting

Summer to find out how she was doing while working on her to cater and host his party.

Summer arrived at Radcliffe's in a great mood. The European elegance of the decor with its Old World oil paintings with spotlights, mahogany woodwork, gleaming crystal chandeliers, and pristine white tablecloths and red brocade-covered dining chairs helped. So did the fact that the Li'l Green Monster had taken a hike.

She was determined not to let whatever it was that was causing her strange reaction to Sin interfere with their friendship. Life was good. To prove her point, Summer purposefully waited for Kerri, her executive chef, who was tugging a resigned head waitress toward her instead of making a fast retreat to her office.

Kerri created pure culinary magic in the kitchen, and didn't cave under pressure. It was a bit of a revelation to see the serious chef turn into a woman consumed with plans over her upcoming wedding. She kept all of them updated—whether they wanted the update or not.

"Good morning, Kerri, Joan," Summer greeted.

"Good morning, Summer." Kerri wore a crisp white chef's uniform, the jacket unbuttoned, and her long auburn hair in its usual knot atop her head. Her round, pretty face beamed.

"Morning, Summer." Head waitress Joan started to move away when Kerri released her arm.

Kerri caught her before she made a step. "Please stay. I'm bursting to tell you about my wedding gown." She waited until Joan faced her. "It's absolutely gorgeous. It was well worth the custom price tag. The crystal beaded detail is exquisite. I'm going in for my final fitting two weeks before the wedding." Kerri's eyes sparkled. "Thomas is going to be speechless when he sees me coming down the aisle."

"I'd like to see that," deadpanned Joan.

"He won't be able to take his eyes off you," Summer quickly interjected, unsure if Joan was being sarcastic or stating fact. With her dry wit, it was difficult to tell. Slim, pretty with a sleek cap of red hair, she was known for her one-liners.

Thomas *was* talkative, perhaps because he was the manager of the shoe department in a retail store. He and Kerri met when she, a confirmed shoeaholic, had gone to a sale. Another romance due to fate.

"Just as long as he can say I do." Kerri's laughter bubbled over with happiness.

Summer smiled softly as she fought against another brief twinge—okay, more than a twinge. Looked like Green Eyes was back from vacation. But she wasn't going to rake herself over the coals again. Her feelings were to be expected with her friends and employees all finding someone to love while she went to bed with the latest industry magazines.

She'd forgive herself for her lapses. She was human.

Joan, who had been looking bored and who made it no secret that she enjoyed men and wasn't ready to settle down to one, suddenly perked up. She moistened her red lips, shifted her weight to lean back on one leg so her generous breasts—which she always said caught men's attention first and she did the rest—jutted forward.

Summer instantly knew Joan's attention had shifted to a man. Her sultry smile was both an invitation and a promise. In the privacy of her home, Summer had tried to copy Joan's expression and always looked as if she had tasted alum.

Since Summer had a strict no-fraternization policy for employees at Radcliffe's, she glanced over her shoulder to see the man who had caught Joan's attention this time.

Sin, a charming grin on his gorgeous bearded face, was heading in their direction. His charcoal-gray double-breasted suit fit his trim body perfectly and made a woman want to investigate what lay beneath. Even happily engaged, Kerri stopped talking.

Sin always had that mesmerizing effect on women. If the incredible face and sexy body didn't get to you, the deep, captivating voice—it flowed over a woman's body and made her think of his strong, possessive hands doing the same thing— would.

To his credit, he didn't exploit the fact that women were drawn to him. He walked with the self-assured grace and power of a healthy animal in complete control of his surroundings.

Although both women had seen him dozens of time, it made no difference. After much thought, Summer had concluded that, no matter how many times the unexpected appearance of something graceful and beautiful crossed your path, you never got used to the sight and were still drawn by its magnificence.

But she knew better than anyone that beneath the gorgeous exterior, Sin was a man you could count on. He was also the man who had taught her to accept that it was all right to have moments of weakness, then get on with her life.

Excusing herself, she met Sin beneath one of the imported crystal chandeliers in the middle of the restaurant. His easygoing expression wasn't fooling her. He wanted answers about her behavior yesterday—which she wasn't about to give him. "Sin, I'm super-busy."

"Hello to you, too."

"The smile won't work on me. Full house tonight with some foreign and state dignitaries on the guest list. Good-bye." She headed for her office, and although she couldn't hear him on the green marbled floor, she knew he was behind her. That pit-bull mentality of his.

He wasn't leaving until he was sure she was all

right, and while she appreciated him caring, this was one secret she wasn't going to share with him. Or anyone. She certainly wasn't going to clarify her comment weeks ago about "makeup sex." As if she knew anything about that. She caught herself before bemoaning something else she'd missed out on. No more pity party for her today. She had a restaurant to run.

Her chin up, she opened the door to her office.

"Glad to see the flowers I sent you last week are holding up well."

Flowers were one of her weaknesses and Sin knew it. But she also knew he hadn't sent them to be manipulative; but simply because he knew she'd enjoy them. That's what made Sin so hard to resist—he had an uncanny sense of timing.

The flowers had arrived the day she had three employees call in sick just as the restaurant opened. They'd scrambled to make adjustments so the customers' dining experience would be just as enjoyable.

When the front door was locked a little after one o'clock the next morning, bone-tired but proud, she'd gone to her office and slipped off her heels. They'd had a great night. Seeing the stunning arrangement of exotic flowers in a profusion of colors on her desk had brought a smile to her face.

No matter what, life goes on. You either meet the challenge or cave.

"Go bother some athlete or executive."

"I'd much rather be here with you." Smiling, he stepped around her and sprawled elegantly in one of the comfortable Queen Anne chairs covered in rich ecru imported silk from France.

She hadn't been sure about the final decision on decorating the office or the restaurant after consulting with a decorator and her aunt. She'd wanted herself and her customers to feel as if they'd stepped back into an earlier time of Old World elegance and charm, and she'd been so afraid she'd end up with neither.

It was Sin who found her with her head down on the beach behind her aunt and uncle's estate, her head full of color schemes, fabric swatches, fixtures, wood finishes. He'd told her to trust her own judgment. She'd done so, and couldn't be happier with the way her office and the restaurant had turned out.

His influence had been felt even before then. If not for him, she might not have become a master chef. When she'd gone to Paris to study, she'd become homesick within a week. Sin had picked up on it when he'd called to check on her. The next day when she arrived home from class at her apartment, he and her aunt were there.

They'd stayed for a week, and when they left, he reminded her that he would always be a phone call away. She'd never forgotten and had called on him more than anyone in her family. Never once had he seemed to mind.

If there was one person in the world who could get her to do almost anything, it was the sinfully handsome man in front of her. Worse, he knew it.

"Sin, I'm extremely busy. So good-bye."

"I really need to talk with you about something vital," he told her. With his uncompromising good looks and sleek build, he always seemed at ease wherever he was. When other men, including C. J. with his broad shoulders, sat in the chair, they always looked a bit out place or uncomfortable. But like a chameleon, Sin adapted to his surroundings.

Summer lifted one naturally arched brow and folded her arms. "Things are always vital with you, Sin."

He leaned back in the chair and crossed one long leg over the other at the ankles, indicating that he had no intention of leaving. "Then we should discuss what I came for so you can get back to running the restaurant."

Up went her other brow. Sin smiled. Summer wrinkled her lips to keep from smiling back. They liked to tease and spar with each other, but today she really didn't have time. Rounding her desk, she took a seat and placed her hands on top of several colorful folders.

"Glad to see your smile is back," he said, the teasing gone from his face.

"Keep it there by leaving," she said.

The corners of Sin's sensual mouth lifted. "What, and miss the pleasure of your incredible company?"

But never the pleasures she unwillingly found herself thinking about. "Laying it on a bit thick, are we?" she asked.

He sat up. "Probably, but I meant what I said."

Her resistance faded just a tad. She felt the odd sensation she'd been feeling more and more lately when Sin gave her a compliment. His opinion of her had always meant a lot. He didn't blow smoke. He associated with some of the wealthiest, most famous people in the world. The phone on her desk rang.

"Yes, Maria," she said on picking up the receiver. "Please tell the Hennessy rep I'll be right out." Summer came to her feet, and so did Sin. "When I get back, I don't expect to see you. Have a pleasurable day."

"Please tell Carlos I always have Hennessy on hand," Sin commented as she passed. "I enjoy having the best."

"You could always tell him on your way out." Opening the door, Summer paused.

He feigned innocence. "I wouldn't dare intrude on a business meeting."

Summer rolled her eyes. "Whatever it is you're trying to get me to do, I'm booked, so take yourself off and worry someone else." The door closed behind her.

"But it's more fun with you." He wondered if she knew how her eyes sparkled when she was about to tear into him. She enjoyed sparing with him as

much as he did with her. There was something about
Summer that always made him want to smile.

Smiling now, Sin retook his seat just as his
iPhone rang. Removing it from the breast pocket of
his suit jacket, he automatically looked at the caller
ID. Every muscle in his body tensed.

He didn't want to answer the call from his sister-
in-law Liz. He didn't want to hear that his brother
Michael had had another episode, or worse, but
love proved stronger than the fear.

He activated the call. "Liz," he said, aware his
voice wasn't quite steady.

"Payton, we were worried for nothing," she said,
the words rushing out with happiness.

Sin leaned his head back against the chair, his
hand remaining clenched on the iPhone. He'd
learned early in life that people made themselves
believe what they wanted when reality was too un-
thinkable. "Are you sure?"

"Positive." Her happy laughter drifted through
the phone. "Things have been going great this past
week. I'm going to prepare Michael's favorite meal
tonight while the boys are at the movies with
friends."

The "boys" were his twin sixteen-year-old nephews. Sin loved and spoiled them. They were bright,
happy, and popular, and they excelled at sports, just
as Michael had predicted when they were born. Sin
hoped and prayed nightly that his brother's other
prediction came true as well.

"I better get ready for work and get out of here before I get caught in the freeway traffic," Liz said. "I just wanted you to know so you wouldn't worry."

Sin wished that was possible. Liz worked part-time at Neiman Marcus's flagship store in downtown Dallas in precious jewels. With Michael's seven-figure income she didn't need to work, but Liz said, since the twins were older and she liked fine jewelry, working at Neiman's part-time was the perfect solution to indulge herself without feeling guilty.

"Good luck with sales today," Sin told her, trying to sound happy, hoping she didn't realize it was forced.

"Thanks. Bye."

"Bye." Sin shut down the cell phone but kept it gripped in his hand. Leaning forward in his chair, he wished he didn't have the churning in his gut that Liz was horribly wrong and that, no matter what any of them did, there was nothing on this earth they could do to avert the disaster headed straight for them.

Thirty minutes later, Summer bid the rep good-bye and headed for her office, well aware that Sin, as usual, had followed his own dictates and remained. The front door was clearly visible from the forty-foot rosewood bar. She'd be angry with anyone else who so blatantly ignored her wishes, but with Sin it was more a case of who could get the other to bend first. She'd long since lost count of who was ahead in the game. It was too much fun.

Today she was definitely going to be the winner. She was too busy for whatever Sin was trying to finagle her into doing. Unlike C. J., who was straightforward, Sin liked to build a case for what he wanted rather than asking straight-out. It wasn't Alex's influence as a lawyer that made Sin that way. More likely it was his days as a star athlete in high school and college. He simply enjoyed competing and emerging victorious.

That wasn't happening today.

Summer reentered her office, determined to get rid of Sin . . . until she saw him leaning forward in the chair, his head and shoulders deeply slumped. Fear had her rushing across the room to stand in front of him.

"Sin?"

Sin, perpetually happy and moving, was as still as a statue. When he looked up, there was such misery in his face that her heart clenched. Without thinking, she knelt down in front of him and covered his clasped fists with her hands. She felt the slight trembling.

Slowly her heart rate returned to normal, her fear receded. She'd been afraid it was his heart. Both her uncle and her cousin, who'd appeared to be healthy, had experienced sudden heart attacks.

She started to ask if he was all right, but clearly he wasn't. She thought of calling C. J., but Sin's hands had closed over hers. He had given comfort to her so often. If she could give in return, that was exactly what she planned on doing.

"Would you go for a walk with me?" he asked, his usually cheerful voice hoarse.

"Yes." Refusing never entered her mind.

He got to his feet, bringing her with him, and started for her door. She needed to grab her cell phone. She was never out of contact with the restaurant. Sin wasn't rushing, but his intent was obvious.

As luck would have it, Daphne, Summer's manager, was entering the restaurant as she and Sin were heading out. They stopped short of bumping into each other. Three months' pregnant, Daphne was late due to an ob-gyn appointment. Sin stepped aside, nodded a greeting, but he didn't release Summer's hand. He knew her staff almost as well as she did.

"Sorry," Daphne said with a smile. "Morning, Sin. Summer."

"Morning, Daphne," Summer greeted as Sin began moving around the other woman. "I'm not sure how long I'll be gone. Please check my appointments and take care of things."

Daphne's gaze flickered to Sin, his face set in grim lines. "Will do."

"Thanks," Summer called as she passed. Sin wasn't moving fast, but he was moving, her hand still in his. Outside, he turned toward Central Park and kept walking.

Chapter 3

Hand in hand they aimlessly walked. Sin didn't know or care where. He just had to keep moving. It was as if he could somehow evade the inevitable if he did. But he couldn't.

None of them could.

His hand flexed, felt Summer's soft and fragile hand, yet somehow he gathered strength from just knowing she was there. He couldn't explain it, just accepted it and was thankful she was there, even as he knew he could never share his family secret with her.

His grip eased, his steps slowed, the tension draining from his body. He stopped beneath the red awning of a coffee shop. "Would you like a cup of tea?"

"That would be nice."

Nodding, his hand sliding around her slim waist, he opened the door. Customers were eating at the small tables, working on computers, reading. There was a line in front of the two cashiers. "Grab us a table."

She hesitated. "Go on. I'm all right." He indicated an empty table in the back, his gaze not meeting hers.

"All right."

Sin watched her move away, the erectness of her posture, the graceful elegance of her slender body. Today she had on a long tangerine-colored cotton dress that swirled around her long legs as she walked, but he knew she kept more elegant clothes in her office to change into before the restaurant opened at 5:00 PM. The color suited her clear complexion.

When she reached for the back of a red padded metal chair facing him, Sin moved to get in line. He didn't want her seeing the lingering shadows in his eyes.

"What'll you have?" asked the young cashier, who looked bored but resigned.

"Earl Grey. Medium cappuccino. Apple Danish." Sin paid for the food, then stepped aside to wait for the harried person behind the counter to prepare his order. Summer always liked Earl Grey. Perhaps because he was born and raised in Dallas, he didn't want tea unless it had sugar, lemon, and lots of ice cubes floating in the glass.

"Thanks." Taking the tray, he joined Summer at the table by the window.

He doubted if many people could have resisted asking questions this long. Not Summer. She was the calmest, most serene, caring person he knew.

"Thank you." She placed the tea bag into the cup of hot water, then eyed the enormous Danish he placed midway between them, and took the plastic fork he handed her. "Pulling out the big guns. You know I have a difficult time refusing pastries. Must be something huge you want from me."

She was going to let him off the hook. No wonder that, in the past few months when things in his life were crazy, being with or talking to Summer had smoothed out the rough edges, even more so than with his two best friends.

"Thank you." He sipped his coffee, knowing she'd understand.

Smiling, she dipped her head slightly and picked up her tea. "This is good. Have you been here before?"

"No." He forked in a bite of Danish although he'd never felt less like eating. At the moment, he needed the normalcy. There was no way he was going to burden anyone else with his family problems. He'd confided in Alex because he was his lawyer and friend. It ended there.

But he also realized Summer had walked away from the restaurant she loved without question or hesitation because he'd asked her to. Leaning back in his chair, he stared across the table at her. "You're an amazing woman."

She lifted a brow in that imperial way of hers. "Tell me something I don't know."

Sin caught himself smiling. He could brood and

worry or he could live each day to the fullest, just as he has always done. Setting the paper cup aside, he braced his folded arms on the table. "I want to have a thank-you party at my place and invite my athlete-clients as well as executives for the merchandise they endorse. I want all of them to have a great time. Give the athletes the best stage to play on, so to speak."

Summer placed her fork on the plate and folded her arms. "It's a wonderful idea. But if you're even thinking of asking me to cater for you, the answer is no. The same goes for catering any more games at your stadium suite. There are dozens of firms you can hire. I can give you a list."

He was already shaking his dark head, his mouth set. "I don't want anyone I don't know. I want someone who can think for themselves and won't call me or my secretary, asking questions they should know. Most important, I don't want there to be any surprises the night of the party." His eyes narrowed. "The last firm that catered at the stadium served finger sandwiches, hot pasta salad, and a fruit and relish tray."

Summer started to shake her head, sure he was joking. "Your suite is filled with men, big men with bigger appetites."

"I told the woman that. She didn't listen. She thought they'd like something light because it was so hot." Sin shook his head in disgust. "As if we were outside instead of in an air-conditioned luxury suite for three hours. I kept apologizing to my guests, and they kept asking about you."

"I'm sorry, Sin. I'll give you the menu of what I serve so they can use it as a guideline," she told him. "Part of going to a ball game is the camaraderie and the good food."

"You understand that." He leaned toward her. "You understand that different aspects have to work together to make any event a success."

She held up both hands, palms-out. "Oh, no, you don't. I'm not the only person in New York who understands that concept. So turn those eyes in another direction."

He frowned. "What?"

Summer rolled hers. Perhaps he did it instinctively, looked at you as if you were the only person who could accomplish what he wanted, made you yearn just the tiniest bit to please him. "I'll e-mail the name of the company Aunt Evelyn uses this afternoon."

"Mrs. Callahan knows what she wants. I don't expect my party to be a bit elegant," he told her earnestly. "If I hire anyone it will just be my misfortune that they'll want to use their ideas and it will end up like nothing I envisioned."

Summer silently admitted he had a point. Too many times if you didn't know exactly what you wanted, or if your ideas weren't in sync with the people you hired, whoever was in charge relied on their own judgment. Sometimes they were able to come to an agreement, but other times it just didn't happen.

While she empathized with Sin, this one time she had to say no. "Sin, Daphne is still having occasional morning sickness. Kerri is getting married in two months, and we have several important group bookings, which always make for a hectic night."

"Daphne is your manager, but your assistant is just as proficient. I already know you have backup for Kerri. For the third year in a row, Radcliffe's received a Triple-A Five Diamond Award for food, service, and decor."

"And I intend to make it four years in a row," she told him.

"You will," he came back instantly. "You have competent, experienced staff who work their tails off because they pride themselves on what they do, they respect and adore you, and they know you work twice as hard. They want to please you and they know you'll accept nothing less than their best."

She picked up her cup of tea. He was right, of course. Her staff was excellent. She just wasn't sure it was wise to spend more time than necessary around him until she again thought of him as just a male friend and not one she was attracted to. "My parents always said, if you weren't going to do your best, there was no point in doing it."

"I couldn't agree more." Sin braced his arms on

the table. "The party has got to click on all cylinders. Some of the athletes and executives came from middle-class or privileged backgrounds, others used their brains or brawn or both to take them to the top of their profession. They're a diverse, interesting group of men and women. There are those with the gift of gab, while others won't know what to say or aren't used to small talk. The right atmosphere will set the tone for the evening."

Summer placed her cup on the table and nodded her understanding, trying not to notice how competent and strong his hands looked. And failing badly.

"Then you're going to have to walk a thin line with elegance—which usually means formal with table menus, designated seating, and place cards."

"Then strike formal." He grinned. "See, I knew you'd understand."

"No."

"Summer, this is one time I really need you."

Her crazy heart thudded. The sincerity in his voice throbbed though her, made her want to do whatever he asked. She gritted her teeth instead. He always tugged at her emotions and now it had gotten worse. She had to remember that other women he'd dated had probably felt the same pull—for all the good it had done them.

Stay strong, Summer.

"There's something else I haven't told you. I need you to be my hostess *and* do the catering." He rushed on, seeing what must have been shocked surprise on her face. "With your innate style and self-assurance, I can't think of anything I'd rather have to guarantee that everything goes off without a hitch."

"Your current girlfriend," she suggested, and winced at the pettiness in her voice.

"I haven't had one of those in a long time," he told her tightly and leaned back in his seat.

Summer frowned at the unexpected abruptness and reminded herself that Sin not having a girlfriend didn't mean she could step into that position. *Friends. Just friends.* "With Alex married and C. J. on his way, I would have thought that you might be thinking more about a permanent relationship."

Ducking his head, he reached for his cup. "Marriage isn't for me. With six offices scattered across the country, I'm on the road too much." He gazed over the top of the cup. "How about you?"

"Me?" she parroted, jerking upright in her seat.

"You, Dianne, and Cicely have become close friends." He frowned and put his cup down. "You dating some guy? Is that why you won't be my hostess?"

As if. "No. Like you, I'm too busy to be in a serious relationship," she told him. *Try* any *relationship.*

"You have to be careful these days, Summer. Some men can't be trusted," he cautioned.

"Stop being overprotective." She threw her hands into the air. "C. J. is bad enough. I don't get into your business with women."

"I told you I'm not dating," he said.

"Excuse me, but I find that difficult to believe."

"Believe it." He shrugged those incredible shoulders. "You're the first and only person I thought of. Maybe that's why I thought of elegance." He said the last words slowly as if realizing it for the first time.

The muscles of her stomach clenched. His words stroked her, made her feel those unfurling emotions again. Tucking her head, she picked up her fork and took another bite of her Danish, hoping it stayed down with the crazy way her stomach was jumping. "Flattery will get you nowhere."

Sin frowned. "It's the truth. Besides helping me, you'll help Radcliffe's. There'll be some important people there, people who can spread the word about Radcliffe's, dine there. You can never be too well known."

Sin had contributed a lot to her success. He'd sent his friends and associates to Radcliffe's the week it opened. He continued to send patrons her way and recommend her restaurant.

Yet if she helped him, she was in danger of becoming more sensually aware of him. They'd have to work closely together, be in contact more than in the past. She wasn't sure that was wise. But more than the risk to herself, she was concerned about those shifting shadows in his eyes. She had the strongest urge to cover his hand with hers again, to pull him into her arms and comfort him as he had done her so many times in the past.

She didn't dare. She had to be smart and logical about this. Being Sin's hostess would be another reminder that there was no one special in her life, and an even bigger and more painful reminder that the man who had awakened her emotions could never be more than a friend.

"Summer, I need you."

Her heart plopped. She was well and truly hooked. Need was a strong inducer. There was no way she could turn her back on him when shadows lurked in his dark eyes, even if there was an emotional risk to herself. Hopefully, planning the party together might keep his mind off whatever he couldn't forget. Sin was a strong, resourceful, self-sufficient man. The problem had to be incalculable.

However, she wasn't about to let him have an easy victory. He wouldn't want that. She picked up her fork. "Catering the type of event you're talking about would in no way compare to feeding the guests at your suite at the stadium."

"Nor would I want it to." Picking up his cup, he sipped. "I want this to be unique and one-of-a-kind."

A tall order in New York, but she'd never considered herself ordinary. She licked the tines of the fork and stared at him. "This kind of party would be very expensive."

He set his cup aside. "I understand and would give you carte blanche as always. I want the best of everything, and that's what you'll bring to this party, along with your unique sense of style."

"I haven't said I'd do it."

"You haven't said you won't." He grinned. "At least not in the last two minutes."

She laughed. He always made her want to laugh with him. Lately there were other things she wanted to do with him, more intimate things, but that would remain her little secret. "You're incorrigible."'

"Does that mean you'll do it?" he asked.

Summer placed her fork on the plate, drawing out the moment although she was sure he already knew the answer as well as she did. "Get ready for your checkbook to take a major hit."

Laughing, he jumped up and pulled her into his arms. "Thank you."

"Stop embarrassing me," she protested, although she had to fight the urge to hug him tighter, to try to completely banish whatever had taken the laughter from his beautiful black eyes. Playfully, she pushed against his muscled chest when he continued to grin down at her.

"Thank you." Still grinning, he placed a ten on the table and reached for her arm. "I'll walk you back."

Outside he frowned on realizing they were several blocks from Radcliffe's. His gaze turned to her slender feet. She had on tangerine-colored flats with a cluster of beads on the toes that were the

exact color of her dress and the small stones dangling from her pierced ears. At least she didn't have
on the high heels she wore during business hours.
Still . . .

His troubled gaze lifted to hers. "You should
have said something."

Her fingertips lightly touched his cheek; then
they were gone. "You needed me and that was more
important. Now, however, please get a cab and let
me have your phone so I can check on my restaurant."

Still feeling the lingering touch of her fingers, he
gave her his phone and waved down a cab. She was
still trying to soothe him. He didn't want to think
about the time she would no longer be in his life.
But that day was coming. Perhaps sooner than he
wanted to admit.

A cab pulled up to the curb just as she finished her
call. Opening the back door for her, he helped
her inside. "Everything all right?" he asked after
he'd given their destination.

"Yes. As you said, I have competent staff." She
gave the iPhone back to him.

"We can discuss the particulars of the party over
breakfast in the morning—if you're free."

"I am, but why the rush?"

He grinned for the sheer pleasure of it. "Because
the party is less than four weeks away."

She gasped. "What?"

He tried to look embarrassed. "You were busy

and I was out of town a great deal, and when I came back C. J. was having problems admitting he was in love . . ." Sin's voice trailed off, and he shrugged. "I never had a chance to ask you until today."

She punched him in the chest. He forgot pretense and pulled her to him. Since the shadows were completely gone from his eyes, she laughed with him.

Sin was smiling as he entered his office. Being with Summer always did that for him. There was something about her beautiful smile, the teasing light in her incredible eyes that banished the shadows and lifted his spirits. Thank goodness whatever was bothering her yesterday was gone.

Rounding his desk he took a seat, reached for his notebook, and saw the picture of his brother and family. His happy spirits plummeted. He picked up the silver frame and stared at Michael, Liz, Jardon, and Jadon on the Orient Express. They'd taken the picture while they were on vacation in Europe two years ago.

Michael was eight years older and the best big brother in the world. He never minded his baby brother tagging alone. He'd helped him learn to ride a bike, throw a football, drive a stick shift, pick up girls.

"Be all right," Sin whispered. Replacing the photograph, he picked up the phone on his desk and punched in his brother's office number. Sin needed to hear Michael's voice. His grip unconsciously tightened as the phone continued to ring. It was 11:43 AM in Dallas. Michael was scheduled to be in his office this morning. "Please be all—

"Hey, what's up, Payton."

The jubilant voice of his brother caused the muscles in Sin's body to slowly relax. "Nothing much. How are things there?"

There was a slight pause. "You aren't checking up on me again, are you?"

Sin heard the slight edge in his brother's voice and accepted the inevitable. "So, I love you and worry about you."

"Love me by not worrying," Michael snapped. "So I forgot a couple of appointments, and let my temper get the best of me with a couple of employees. In ten years of being your second in command, you've never had any concerns. I'm entitled, don't you think?"

"Yes." But they both were afraid to voice the possibility that it could be more than that. "You're entitled."

"Listen, man, I'm all right."

They both desperately wanted to believe that. "You change your mind about meeting me in Phoenix for the All-Star game next Tuesday, then flying with me to LA the next day for the ESPY Awards?"

"I'm pretty busy here" came the quick answer.

They hadn't missed an All-Star game since Sin started Sinclair Management ten years ago. Liz got a huge kick out of meeting the celebrities attending the ESPYs. "My party?"

"Sorry, can't. Besides, you aren't inviting some of our top clients in the area and I don't want them wondering why," Michael explained. "It will help if I'm not there."

They were all excuses. In the past couple of months Michael had started avoiding Sin. They used to talk at least once a week, not simply about the business, but just to shoot the breeze and keep in touch. At one time they were as close as two brothers could be, but since Michael's outburst, they seemed to have grown farther apart.

"I didn't invite them because I didn't want them in my home," Sin finally answered. "Some of our clients have become more of a liability than an asset. Like Glen Atkins."

"I read about him in the *Morning News* this morning," Michael said. "You considering cutting him loose?"

"It crossed my mind," Sin said. "I don't want to do business with a man I dislike on a personal level."

"Still, business relationships are important. Dad used to say that," Michael mused.

Sin's fingers flexed on the phone. "I remember."

Another pause. "I gotta go. Bye."

Sin hung up the phone. Their father had been the best, a good man who loved his family above all else. Yet when he needed them the most, they had let him down. Their mother was dead. Only Sin and his older brother remained, and no matter what, neither of them would ever forget.

He dialed another number. "Dr. Kearns, please. Payton Sinclair calling."

In a matter of moments the doctor was on the line. "Payton, how are things going?"

Sin briefly shut his eyes. "It's Michael. I think it's started."

Summer celebrated those days at Radcliffe's when no catastrophes occurred because she knew there would be days when things went wrong. Monday night was one of those times.

"I'm sorry, Summer," came the brisk voice of Frank Hollis, the delivery driver of her van to the Second Chance, the shelter C. J. had founded and continued to be a major sponsor for.

Sitting behind her office desk a little after eleven, she quickly dismissed the man's apology. "Frank, this isn't your fault. You didn't plan on dislocating your shoulder."

"It was supposed to be *touch* football," he said, anger creeping into his deep voice. "I think my brother-in-law 'forgot' on purpose. His day is coming. I can guarantee it."

Summer didn't have a shred of doubt that Frank would make good on his threat. Six feet tall, 230 pounds, and built like a wrestler, he had a glint in his eyes that said he was a man you didn't mess with. And it had nothing to do with the tattoos that covered his body, his nose ring, or the kick-butt Harley he often rode without a helmet.

"I tried to find another commercial driver to take my place, but they're all busy. I know you're counting on me," he went on to say. "I'd come anyway, but my wife took the keys to my truck."

"And I'm keeping them until the doctor says you can drive," Summer heard a female voice say.

"Don't worry, Frank. The food will get delivered," she assured him.

"But how?" he questioned. "No one at the restaurant has a commercial driver's license, and it's too late to hire anyone."

All true. "I'll think of something. Good night and get some rest."

"'Night, Summer, and I'm sorry for letting you down."

"You did no such thing," Summer insisted. "In the past year, you've never missed a delivery to Second Chance, no matter what the weather. I don't know what we would have done without you."

"I know what it is to be hungry," he said slowly. "The shelter gave me a place to start to heal, to get my life and my wife back. Ain't nothing I wouldn't do to help the shelter, C. J., or you."

"I know, Frank. I'll take care of things. Goodbye." Summer hung up the phone wishing she knew how. There wasn't enough room in her refrigerator to keep the food until the morning. The thought of the men in the shelter going hungry sent a sinking feeling in her stomach. She'd call C. J., but he had left on a business trip that morning.

There was only one solution.

Opening the drawer of her desk she picked up the keys to the van, stood, and headed for the kitchen. She had her commercial driver's license. She tried not to think that she'd never driven the van in New York traffic this late at night.

As usual the kitchen was full of activity. It didn't matter that the last guest had been seated. Radcliffe's was a dining experience; people lingered over their wine, their dessert and coffee, conversation, each other.

"Charles," she called as the door swung shut behind her. "Is everything boxed and ready to go?"

The slender young man with dreads nodded. "Sure thing, Ms. Radcliffe. Frank running late?" His voice held a strong hint of his Jamaican homeland.

"He's not coming. I'm taking the food."

Quiet dropped over the kitchen. Joan, who had been heading out with two desserts on her deck tray, paused and backed up.

"Perhaps you should call someone." Kerri paused in adding garnish to the grilled salmon.

"I'm perfectly capable of driving the van," Summer said, not quite sure she wasn't trying to reassure herself. Unfortunately, a lot of New York drivers didn't follow traffic rules or etiquette in the daytime. At night, they could be maniacal.

Charles reached behind his back to untie his

apron. "I'll go with you. C. J.'s shelter is in a safe area, but you have to get to it."

"You're needed here. I'll check with Daphne and then I'm gone. I just wanted to make sure everything was ready to go." Summer turned. "Joan, I'm sure our guests would appreciate their desserts."

The waitress didn't move. "You shouldn't go by yourself."

"I appreciate the concern. I really do, but I can handle this." She kept the waitress's gaze until the other woman turned for the door. Summer followed, telling herself again that she could do this. She didn't have a choice. She wasn't taking anyone that was needed at the restaurant.

Chapter 4

"You can do this. You can do this." Summer gripped the steering wheel and repeated the litany every time a car cut in front of her, every time someone blew their horn because she was driving below the speed limit, every time she got the finger.

When she finally reached Second Chance and pulled around to the back of the well-lit one-story brick building, it took a few moments to unclamp her hands from the steering wheel. She leaned her head back and closed her eyes.

The knock on the window caused her to jump, her heart to leap into her throat. She jerked her head around to see Sin, arms akimbo, staring at her with a hard frown on his face. He wore a New York Yankees baseball cap, jeans, and a dark navy blue polo shirt. Opening the door, she got out of the van. "What are you doing here?"

"I don't know whether to be proud of you or shake you for being so careless."

From the glint in his eyes, she thought it was the

latter. "Frank dislocated his shoulder, and there was no one else."

"You could have called me."

"Frankly, that never entered my mind."

His jaw clenched. His eyes narrowed. "Open the back."

She didn't think, she just hurried after him and caught his arm, felt the bunched muscles beneath. She hadn't meant the words to sting. "I'm used to taking care of my own problems. I can't call you or C. J. if my life takes a bump."

"What if you had a flat? What if some psycho tried to get into the van at a stoplight? Or you had an accident?" Sin barked out the questions.

He was angry because he'd been worried. "I thought of everything you just asked me and more. I was scared or terrified most of the drive here, but I made it and tomorrow the thirty-odd men living here will have a good meal because I didn't let that fear stop me."

"Summer—" He pulled her to him, blew out a breath, held her.

She wasn't sure which one of them was trembling. Perhaps they both were. She looped her arms around his waist, pressed her forehead against the softness of his beard, and gave in to the pleasure of just being held by him.

"You wouldn't answer your phone. I kept calling."

She heard the strain in his voice, and felt even worse for scaring him. "It's not synced to the van. I didn't want to search for it in my purse and have an accident," she said, the warmth of his body slowly erasing the fear. Unconsciously, she rubbed her cheek against his. It always amazed her how soft his beard was. "I'm sorry." Then another thought occurred. She pushed out of his arms, almost instantly missing the feeling of safety, of warmth. "How did you know where to find me?"

His hand brushed the long, curly black strands of hair from her forehead, the gesture tender and familiar. She shivered. This time for an entirely different reason than fear. "I realized we hadn't set a time or place for breakfast and called the restaurant. When I asked for you, they put me through to Daphne."

"Who told you I had taken Frank's place against her advice," Summer guessed.

"She was worried."

"And you came charging to my rescue." Summer said the words teasingly, but it felt nice to have him there. She shouldn't be greedy wanting more.

"And found you were doing just fine." He reached for the keys in her hand. "Let's get the food unloaded." He handed her a container labeled BREAD and effortlessly lifted a larger, heavier one labeled MEAT.

She blew out a breath and curved her arms around the plastic container. "Yeah. Once I got my fingers unstuck from the steering wheel."

In the bright floodlight stationed at the corner

and apex of the building, his brows bunched and he stared at her a long time. "You didn't turn around despite your fear. You're an amazing woman."

Her stomach dipped. "You said that this morning."

"Some things bear repeating." He walked toward the back door of the one-story structure. Summer followed with a huge grin on her face.

Thirty minutes later, after they'd unloaded the food and visited with the director and counselor who lived at the residence, they were back outside. Sin handed Summer the keys and opened the driver's door. "You did it once. Going back should be a breeze."

"You aren't going to drive?" she questioned.

"You made it here. You can make it back." He nodded toward the seat. "Get in. I need my beauty sleep."

Making a face, she climbed inside. He was joking, of course. Sin was as down-to-earth as they came. Besides, if he was any better looking, he'd stop traffic. By the time Sin had fastened his seat belt, she had put the van into gear. "Thank you. If C. J. had been here, once he stopped fussing, he would have driven me back."

Sin leaned back against the seat. "As much as I hate to think about it, you might need to make this run again."

She stopped at the end of the driveway. "And just

like when you taught me how to water-ski. The more I do it, the better I'll become. You always told me the only way to conquer my fears was to face them."

He tugged on the brim of his cap. "Yeah."

Summer frowned at him. "Sin?"

"Traffic's clear." He hadn't been able to hide the mockery in his voice. He'd honestly believed that until four months ago. He'd thought he and Michael might get a pass, but it wasn't shaping up that way. He'd pushed the possibility of one or both becoming ill to the back of his mind, and gone on with his life. That wasn't possible any longer. Dr. Kearns had laid it on the line earlier today.

"We better get going," Sin finally said. "I know you called Daphne, but your employees are probably still anxious to see you."

Summer cautiously pulled into the street. "So where are we meeting for breakfast, and what time?"

She wasn't going to push. She was letting him off again. No wonder he liked being around her. "Whatever you'd like. My first appointment is at eleven. I'm working with a few colleges to help their athletes remain in school and academically eligible to play."

"Which, if the news is right about payoffs, bribes, and the failure of the education system, can't be easy."

Sin noted she drove five miles below the speed limit with both hands on the steering wheel, but at least she wasn't gripping it. She might have scared him spitless, but she had done well. Once he'd held her, known she was all right, he had been able to breathe easier.

"It's not," he finally answered. "Temptation is out there for the best players, plus it's easy to let their egos get too big."

"With playing so many games and the practice it entails, it must be difficult for many of them to keep their grades up." Her speed increased as she passed a car. "I doubt if a lot of non-athletes could keep up their schedule and continue to have good grades."

She understood. He might have known. She'd worked hard for her success as well. No one had handed Summer Radcliffe a pass. "I helped set up a counseling and tutoring program, got needed funding and sponsors. They also have mentors they can talk to. Men and women who know what the students are going through."

"Having someone who understands to talk to helps when life knocks you down." She gripped the steering wheel as she hit the Brooklyn Bridge.

He watched her swallow. She was thinking of her parents. His hand briefly covered hers. "Yes."

"I've been going over things about the party." She turned. "I need to come over and see your place. I haven't been there in a while."

"Anytime. If our schedules don't match, I'll let the housekeeper know you're coming."

She tossed him a grin. "Housekeeper. Nice. I have a cleaning lady twice a week, the same with C. J. and Alex."

He shrugged carelessly. "I'm a worse housekeeper than I am a cook, and that's saying something."

"Your mother let you and Michael off the hook with cooking, huh?"

"She really took good care of us. Spoiled us," he finished softly. She deserved so much more than the lousy hand she had been dealt, and so did his father.

"From the sound of your voice, you spoiled her as well," Summer said.

"Dad, Michael, and I would plan for weeks what to get her, how to surprise her—which seemed to get harder with each passing year—on her special days and at Christmas." Through the years he had ruthlessly hung on to those precious memories. He knew how shattering it was when you didn't have them. "She always said she appreciated the gifts we gave her, but we were her true gifts, her treasures. I never knew how blessed I was to have such great parents until I was older."

"I hear you. You sort of take them for granted when you're growing up. I remember Mom and Dad liked to dance." Summer eased to a stop at a signal, a smile playing at the corners of her mouth. "When I was little, Daddy would hold me in his arms and all three of us would dance together. I'll never forget those moments with them."

Sin glanced at her, studied the enticing tilt of her mouth at the corner, her sharp cheekbones. She was a striking woman, but more than that, she was a woman who didn't give up. He was proud that she could look back on those times with her parents with pride. The sadness would always be there for their passing, but she knew they would have wanted her to have a full life.

His parents had wanted the same thing for their sons, but it wasn't going to happen. Before the oppressing sadness could swamp him, he thought of the good times. "Mom and Dad liked to dance as well. At my junior dance, they owned the dance floor."

"That explains why their son is no slouch on the dance floor." The traffic light changed to green and she pulled off. "Will there be dancing at your party?"

"I hadn't thought about it," he answered.

A smile touched her lips. "We all kept the floor hot at Alex and Dianne's wedding. It was great."

"Would you like there to be dancing?" Sin asked, remembering that he'd enjoyed holding her, feeling the slight weight of her body against his, hearing her laughter in his ear. He smiled at the memory.

"It's your party, so it's what you want." Putting on her signal, she pulled into the alley behind her restaurant. "One thing you won't have to think about if you do go informal is having a cloakroom for the women, and the women won't have to think about outdressing the other women."

Sin sat up, a scowl on his handsome bearded face. "Why do women pull that crap?"

Summer switched off the engine before answering, "Because it makes a woman feel powerful if she's the best dressed, has the most diamonds in the room."

Sin snorted. "If she were powerful, she wouldn't care what others thought." He looked at her. "You'd never pull that stunt. You know who you are."

"Mother always said, if you had to make yourself be seen, the only person who cared was you, so it wasn't worth the effort," Summer said softly.

"If she was as beautiful as you, she didn't have to do much but breathe."

Summer's eyes widened. She probably thought he was snowing her again. For some odd reason her reaction irritated him. All she had to do was look in the mirror. "Come on, let's go inside and reassure everyone."

"We haven't decided on where to eat," she reminded him.

"Would Bailey's on East Fifty-seventh Street at nine on be all right?" he asked when he met her at the front of the van. "They serve an all-American breakfast, the service is good, and so is the food."

"Bailey's at nine it is."

After a restless night of thinking about Sin, Summer slowly walked down the crowded street toward Bailey's. She was so wrapped up in her thoughts she didn't pay any attention to the designer boutiques. Unfortunately, she wasn't any closer to figuring out why this crazy awareness, this unexpected awakening of Sin, had suddenly appeared.

Maybe it was because she was so desperate to be wanted that she had fixated on the most eligible bachelor she knew. If that was so, at least she had good taste. Sin was drop-dead gorgeous with a sexy smile and toned body that promised untold pleasures. She might not have any sexual experience, but she instinctively knew he would go the distance in pleasing a woman.

Or perhaps these new feelings were happening because she'd had a crush on him when she was eighteen. She figured out in Paris that part of the infatuation was due to how sensitive and caring he was after she'd lost her parents. Thank goodness, the crush was over by the time she returned to New York, and she'd gone on with her life.

Now, if she could just get her mind and body to get over him again, she'd be a lot happier.

Or would she?

That was her problem as well. She really didn't know what she wanted.

One moment she embraced her new feelings for Sin, the next she wished them away. It was scary and exhilarating. She'd put more thought into what she wore to meet him today than ever before. She wanted him to notice her as a woman.

Not a good sign.

Absently, she brushed back the wisps of hair that escaped from her braided twist, sending her hammered sterling earrings jingling, the three matching bracelets on her arm doing the same thing. The turquoise stones perfectly matched the predominant color in her multicolored wrap dress, which stopped above her knees. Cicely's blog said the right clothes made a woman feel more confident. If ever there was a day Summer needed confidence, it was today

She wasn't sure she was ready to see Sin again, but she didn't have a choice. Besides, she wasn't the type to run from an obstacle or bury her head in the sand.

In front of the restaurant, she glanced through the plate-glass window and saw the man who heated her body, made her crave what she couldn't have. Sin waved, flashed a grin that made her stomach do a nosedive. She waved back, swallowed, and continued toward the front door, her pace even slower.

She needed to figure out what she wanted and fast. She wasn't like her head waitress, Joan. Summer didn't know how to flirt. And even if she did, if her overtures toward Sin were unwanted, it would embarrass both of them and ruin their friendship. Nothing was worth that.

"I'll get that door for you."

Startled, Summer glanced up to see a clean-shaven man in his midthirties wearing a dark navy suit, red silk tie, and crisp white shirt. She'd been so lost in her thoughts she hadn't seen him. "Sorry. I didn't mean to block the entrance."

The man grinned. "Don't be. This may be my lucky day."

She almost rolled her eyes. Instead she lifted her sunglasses on top of her head. You'd think men would come up with new pickup lines. "Thank you."

"The pleasure is all mine," he said, his tone suggestive as he followed her into the restaurant. "If you aren't meeting anyone, I'd like to buy you a cup of coffee."

Summer paused and glanced over her shoulder at the man. He was handsome enough to ask out a woman he didn't know, but there was also a self-assured tilt to his too-wide mouth. He didn't expect her to say no, but if she did, she'd be forgotten within the hour.

She'd never be that desperate. "No, thank you."

He smiled and reached into the inside pocket of his jacket. "My name is Jason Dean. I work on Wall Street. Call me if you change your mind."

He was arrogant and stupid if he thought all he had to do to get a woman was mention where he worked.

"She won't." Sin crumpled the card with one hand, and took Summer's arm with the other. Completely dismissing the man, Sin turned away. "Our table is waiting."

Summer let Sin lead her away for two very good reasons. One, she was too annoyed at him to speak, and two, the stunned, priceless look on the other man's face. What woman in her right mind would want him when a man as gorgeous as Sin was waiting for her?

Sin reached a table for two and pulled out a chair. "You're as stiff as a board. Before you blast me with both barrels, I know you can take care of yourself."

"Then why?" she asked, remaining standing. "He's not the first guy to try and pick me up. If you don't learn how to hold your own in New York, you're trampled into the ground."

"Not around me, they aren't," Sin came back.

She rolled her eyes. "Because, as I told you, you and C. J. are always hovering and glaring."

"We care about you," Sin told her. "You can tell the guys who are out for only one thing. No one is going to hurt you if I can help it."

Although she hadn't needed it, she was ridiculously pleased that he wanted to protect her. Too pleased.

"He annoyed the hell out of me." Sin glared back toward the door. "Too cocky and too many teeth."

Summer glanced around. The man was gone. "Guess he decided to eat someplace else."

Sin snuck a look at Summer and tried to calm his unreasonable anger. Summer was right. She could take care of herself, but that knowledge hadn't stopped him from intervening. He'd stepped way over the bounds of being protective. He wasn't sure where the fierce possessiveness had come from. He'd never been that way about a woman. There had been no reason. He'd known since he was twenty-one that no woman would share his life.

"I'll restrain myself in the future," he said, trying to tease her into a good mood.

"See that you do."

Finally taking a seat, she pulled out a purse hook from her satchel, attached it to the table, then looped the wide turquoise leather strap over the double hook. She wouldn't look at him.

He'd embarrassed her. He wasn't sure what had come over him. He held out the crumpled card. "I should have let you have the satisfaction of telling him off."

"Yes, you should have, or at least let me give his card back to him." She placed her napkin in her lap. "Since you didn't, you can get rid of the card and I'll forget your bad behavior."

"Deal." He pulled out his chair.

"You ordered juice and coffee. I guess we should ask for menus."

He grinned. "No need. I took care of that as well. I ordered your favorites. French toast, soft scrambled eggs, turkey links, fried potatoes, sweet roll basket."

Summer picked up her orange juice. Ice cubes clinked. "No wonder you're so popular with the women. You anticipate their every need."

"I told you, I'm too busy to date anymore."

Summer stared at him over the rim of her glass. So he had. In the past, when she teased Sin about his long list of women, he'd have some witty comeback. Lately that hadn't been the case. Strangely, she'd never seen Sin with a woman he was dating. When he ate at the restaurant, it was business. The same when she catered at his Yankee Stadium suite. Stranger still because women couldn't keep their eyes off Sin. He could have his pick.

"What?" he asked.

"Nothing." She tilted her glass. If it was a woman that was bothering him, Summer didn't want to know about it. She was not dealing with any more jealousy, especially for a man who called her a friend.

"Here's your food," the waitress said, placing the large platter before them. "Anything else?"

"Summer?" Sin asked

"I'm fine," Summer said, noting the woman hadn't taken her eyes off Sin. It was always that way when they were out, and he never seemed to notice.

"Thanks. That's all for now." Sin sent the woman a brief smile. "I really appreciate your help."

"I hope you feel the same way when you get my bill," Summer said, then tucked her head to bless their food. Lifting her head, she picked up her knife and fork. "Did you decide to take my suggestion and go informal?"

"Yes, but I still want a bit of a wow factor." His

sensual lips curved. "I *am* known for bringing the best of the best together."

The man had the most beautifully shaped lips. Summer mentally shook herself. "What kind of theme do you want?"

Sin paused in reaching for the maple syrup. "Theme? It's just a party to thank my clients."

"First lesson on entertainment, especially in New York, no party is ever 'just' a party. You had a casino theme for C. J.'s party."

"That was a natural," Sin confessed with a grin. "We had a great time in New Orleans and Vegas."

"None of you would say anything about the trips, just grinned whenever anyone asked." Her brow lifted. "And what happens in New Orleans and Vegas . . ."

"Exactly." He picked up his maple syrup pitcher.

She forked in a bite of French toast. "Delicious. You get points for selecting a great place to eat. Now, where were we?"

"Theme." Sin liberally poured the syrup over his short stack. "Stop eyeing my pancakes."

"I don't know why you drown them in syrup until you can't taste the pancakes," she said.

"Blame it on my Texas roots." Sin cut into his thick slice of hickory ham. "If they could make biscuits here like my mother used to make, they'd have a line out the door."

Summer picked up her juice. "And you can't cook one edible dish."

He chuckled. "I made oatmeal last week."

Summer lifted a brow. "Instant, no doubt, and you probably threw it out after one bite."

Sin's lips twitched. "The phone rang and I forgot to stir the stuff."

"It happens to the best of cooks." A smile curved Summer's lips. "Your talents lie elsewhere."

Sin paused, straightened. His eyes narrowed. "I told you I don't date that much."

"I wasn't referring to your dating." Perhaps she'd teased him too much—and what did that say about her?

"Sorry. I guess this party has me a little tense." Sin went back to eating.

Summer didn't believe him for a second, but she let it go. Obviously something was bothering him. It disturbed her that he wouldn't let her help.

She finished her meal in silence, then pushed her plate away and reached into her large bag for a notebook and pen. She liked taking notes the old-fashioned way. She didn't have to worry about a virus or an outlet. "We can come back to theme. So it's definitely informal."

"Informal with a wow factor."

Now she was the one who frowned. "You're really cutting it close. Wow factors take more time to accomplish."

"If I'm asking too much—"

She held up her hand. Hopefully dealing with the party would take his mind off whatever put those shadows in his eyes, and help her get back to normal with him. She'd finally decided that was what she wanted. "I'll make it happen. How many people do you plan to invite?"

"Fifty or so," he answered slowly.

"Have you made a guest list?"

"I'm working on it, but I've already asked some people," he replied.

She nodded. "How many are definite?"

"Maybe ten or so?" he answered, not pleased by the way she was looking at him. He'd seen that look on people across the negotiating table. He wasn't giving her the answers she wanted.

Summer placed her leather-bound notebook on the table. "Sin, parties, the ones that are business-related, are successful because a lot of behind-the-scenes work goes on beforehand. You have no theme, don't know how many people are coming to an informal party with a wow factor. Without that basic knowledge I can't prepare the food or have the proper seating. You have a beautiful penthouse, but there aren't enough seats for fifty people if they all decide to show up."

It bothered him that he had disappointed her. "I'll make a list today."

The waitress approached the table. "Anything else?"

"No, thank you." Summer picked up her pad and pen as the woman cleared the table. Her expression was definitely not as friendly. Sin had made another conquest without even trying.

"While you're at it, think of the theme which will be carried though with the floral arrangements, the linen, and the food. You want people who walk through your door to feel welcome, at ease, and get that wow all at once."

Sin sat back in his chair with a frown. "I never thought of all you had to think about and do when you catered for me at the stadium."

"And you weren't supposed to," she told him. "That's why you hired me, so you could concentrate on your clients and guests."

"They always noticed when you weren't catering," he told her honestly. He did as well. It wasn't just the food; he liked having her there. "You want to catch a game the next time the team's in town? No catering."

"Thanks, but I won't have the free time." She reached for her purse. "While you're making the list today, decide if you want to send Evites or invitations through the mail or just call. Since we're going informal, you can get away with calling your clients, but the business execs need invitations to check their calendars. You need to get on people's schedules. We need a minimum of two weeks for RSVPs—and we're cutting it close—to have a firm number so I can order the party rental things."

He frowned. "Rental things?"

"Linens, tables, chairs, service ware, plates, glasses—I'd go on, but you looked shocked enough." She came to her feet and he stood with her. "Call me with the list, the theme, and your decision about the invitation today. Menu ideas."

He rubbed the back of his neck. "I sort of thought you'd do everything."

Summer slung her satchel strap over her shoulder. "This is your party. It should reflect you, your personality, your business success, not me."

"What's wrong with elegant and beautiful?" he asked.

She blinked. Stared at him.

Looking entirely too pleased with himself, he reached out one finger and lifted her chin to close her mouth. "Never thought you'd be at a loss for words. You are beautiful and elegant and intelligent." Tossing some bills on the table, he led her from the restaurant. "I'll call you with the information today."

She barely kept eye contact with him. Her stomach was doing a rumba. Her decision about friends-only hadn't lasted an hour. Seemed her body had other ideas. "Good-bye, Sin."

"Bye, Summer."

Clutching the satchel to her, Summer continued down the street, still feeling the tingling sensation of Sin's touch, recalling the sincere way he looked at her when he called her beautiful.

"Watch out!"

Summer jerked to a stop to see a bicyclist give a finger to a cabdriver and the driver enthusiastically return the favor. She crossed the street felling a bit off balance. She had better be the one to watch out.

She'd embarrass them both if she wasn't careful. And she was always careful.

Chapter 5

Shortly after three, Summer was working on the payroll when her private line rang. She continued to add the column of figures on her calculator. Behind schedule, she didn't even glance at the phone.

She'd just spent the last two hours, as she did every day, preparing the three six-layer lemon coconut cakes for the dessert menu. Only she knew the recipe. She'd shared some of her recipes with her chefs, but never the cake recipe she and her mother had developed together. It might make her day full, but she liked baking.

The cake was becoming so popular that guests were reserving slices when they made their dinner reservations. When the three cakes were gone, they were gone, and that usually happened a couple of hours into dinner service.

The phone rang again, and again it was ignored.

She needed to get the figures to her accountant before five. It would help if she stopped making mistakes. Thinking about the reason only made things worse. *My attraction to Sin*. The phone rang for the third, then fourth time.

She jerked up the phone. "Radcliffe's."

"Is that you, Summer? It's Krystal from C. J.'s bar, Callahan's."

"Hello, Krystal. This is Summer."

"I hope I didn't catch you at a bad time."

Depends. "What's up?"

"I guess you heard that the employees at the bar are giving C. J. and Cicely their engagement party at Callahan's."

"Yes. C. J. told us Sunday. That's nice of you." Summer entered another figure. "He said it was a week from Saturday."

"Yes, seven PM," Krystal said. "We've already posted signs saying the bar will be closed for a private party, and called in friends to help cook and serve."

"Seems as if you have everything in order." Summer hit TOTAL, stared at the amount on her calculator, and knew she'd have to add the column of figures for the third—or was it the fourth?—time. "C. J. and Cicely are looking forward to it."

"What about his mother?"

Her mind on the payroll, Summer couldn't think of a reply fast enough.

"So, Sam was right," Krystal went on to say. "He remembers the boss's mother the day she came in when C. J. and Cicely first met. Sam showed me the magazine article Cicely wrote with C. J.'s mother and sister on the cover. His mother is high society, and we plan to serve hamburger sliders and onion rings."

"C. J.'s parents love him and Cicely. They'll be pleased with whatever you serve," Summer said. "I've been to affairs where they served mini cheeseburgers."

"How about what their friends and other relatives will think?" Krystal asked, obviously worried. "None of us want to embarrass the boss or Cicely. We just thought it would be special to serve the food she first ate here."

"It is. Both of them appreciate the gesture," Summer answered truthfully, placing a folder over the calculator. She'd have to deal with it later. "The evening is to celebrate their commitment."

"But food is important," Krystal said. "Cicely probably has some fancy friends as well. Maybe we shouldn't have done this."

"No, stop that right now," Summer said, meaning it. "You love C. J., and you want what's best for him. He and Cicely know and appreciate that. It will be the first social event after their engagement and will have a special meaning to them. They're looking forward to it."

"We don't want to embarrass him or Cicely," she repeated, her voice miserable

Summer tried to stop herself, but the words spilled out. "Why don't I prepare a few tidbits to add to the menu?"

"You'd do that? You'd help us?"

Summer heard other, excited voices in the background. Suspicion entered her mind. "Krystal, did you just play me?"

There was another pause. "We're sorry, Summer. We didn't know what else to do," she finally said. "We looked up some of the names on the Internet that C. J. and Cicely gave us. We almost fainted."

Summer could understand their intimidation. Opening night at Radcliffe's, she'd been so nervous she'd thrown up. Her aunt and uncle, her cousins, C. J., Ariel, and their brother, Paul, and his wife, and Sin had been there with praise, hugs, and support. They'd helped her get through the evening.

"They aren't used to eating onion rings and sliders," Krystal went on to say.

"Then they might enjoy a change," Summer said, then went for broke. "How did you plan to decorate the place? Invite guests?"

"Balloons and streamers probably. C. J. and Cicely said that's another memory. They're going to invite people. Cicely wanted us to know how many people to expect so we could prepare food and know who is on the guest list," Krystal said.

C. J.'s mother had probably needed another drink on hearing about the balloons and streamers. Not to mention the fact that there would be no formal invitations. There wasn't enough time. She loved her children, but she believed in things being a certain way and wasn't above telling you if they weren't. "I'll help in any way I can."

"Thank you. You were our only hope. We didn't want to think of what we'd do if you turned us down, but you've always been so nice. You're just like one of the guys."

That was her—one of the guys. "If I can't bring the food, I'll have it delivered."

"You're coming, aren't you?" Panic entered Krystal's voice. "Sin said you were coming."

Summer's shoulders snapped back. "When did you talk to Sin?"

"He called about an hour ago to see if we needed any help with anything," Krystal related. "As best man, he said it was his duty to help financially and in any other way to ensure things went smoothly. Gee, that is one fine man. I drool every time I see him. I just want to jump—sorry."

"No problem." Summer had begun to have similar naughty thoughts. "I have to go now, but if you can meet me at my office around eleven tomorrow, we can go over things. We don't have much time."

"I'll be there. Thank you."

"See you tomorrow."

"Bye, Summer, and thanks."

A little after five that afternoon, Summer stood in front of the floor-length mirror in her office and checked her appearance. Thankfully, she'd finally finished the payroll and messengered it over to her CPA. Now all she had to think about was Radcliffe's.

She'd changed into an above-the-knee, long-sleeved red jersey dress with a boat neck that left the top of her shoulders bare. The dress was elegant without being flashy or over-the-top. She didn't want to distract from the dining experience as she moved around the restaurant talking with customers, ensuring their dining experience was everything they expected or, on rare occasions, helping serve if they became backed up in the kitchen.

She'd just turned away from the mirror when there was a knock on her door. "Come in."

The door opened and the last person she expected entered with a smile, then came to a dead stop. Sin whistled. "Maybe we should go formal, and you could wear that dress."

Summer was glad she'd yet to put on her heels. Her knees felt a little shaky as she kept walking to her desk. Bad. Very bad. "Thanks. What brings you here?"

Stopping in front of her desk, he placed a neatly printed sheet of paper on her blotter. "Twenty-five athletes and five executives have confirmed. Seven executives will have to get back to me, and before you say anything, I told the executives that they would receive a formal invitation within five to ten days."

Impressed and glad to be sitting, Summer slipped her feet into her heels and picked up the list. "I'm impressed. You even have their profession by each name. Most of your guests seem to play football or basketball, with baseball running a distant third. You have quite a diverse group."

Sin folded his arms. "It would be bigger if I tried to invite all the clients that could come or that I'd want to invite."

"Won't those not invited feel slighted?" she asked.

"Eight of my baseball clients have games that weekend. The NBA hasn't started yet, but some of my clients are on vacation. Training camp for NFL has just started and they're just as scattered. My four hockey clients will be in Montreal." He blew out a breath. "You met my latest client, Cameron McBride, at Dianne and Alex's wedding. Wish he could come, but NASCAR is still going strong."

"I know. I was in the bar last Sunday and saw him take the checkered flag," Summer told him. "The TV camera panned to his wife and son. They were ecstatic, of course."

Sin grinned. "He's in high demand, but he has a level head on his shoulders. My lone tennis client can't make it because she has a training camp for underprivileged children that weekend," Sin went on to say. "My golf clients are also iffy due to other engagements, but I think we'll end up with the fifty I told you."

"I never knew you had such a varied list of clients."

"And growing," he answered proudly. "Why do you think I have six offices?"

"All the more reason not to alienate those who

can't make it this time." She studied the list again. "Perhaps you should consider having something in the winter. You could announce it early so it could be on their calendar."

Moving a thick ledger aside, he sat on the corner of her desk. "Good idea, but let's get though this one first."

Summer leaned back in her chair. He was too close, too overpowering, smelled too tempting. "Theme."

He leaned over and grinned. "Western, and we'll serve real Tex-Mex, not what people think is Tex-Mex." He blew out a disgusted breath. "I went with a scout to Mexico and they served hot shrimp cocktails. Who in their right mind serves hot shrimp cocktails?"

Her lips twitched as she reached for her notebook. Sin liked food and had definite ideas on what he wanted. "That's a great idea. Most people already have cowboy boots or hats. Evites with western-theme graphics will be easy to do."

"Don't worry about the printed invitations," he told her and pulled out a business card. "I do a lot of business with this company. Just tell them what you need and they'll print them and mail them."

Summer frowned. "You've been busy."

"And you're going to be busier, I hear."

Her frown deepened. "What?"

"Volunteering to bring food to the engagement party and help with decorations."

She fiddled with a pen on her desk. "They needed my help."

"And you'd never turn down a friend."

"No. I suppose Krystal told you," she guessed.

He nodded. "She called to let me know you'd volunteered so I shouldn't worry. I was a bit annoyed until I looked down at my list and realized I had done the same thing." He drew a lean finger down her cheek. "As a friend, I understand your loyalty; as the best man, I appreciate you; and as a client, I wouldn't have expected anything less from you."

He stood. "So, what can I do to help with the engagement party of my best friend and my own wow party?"

Still feeling the little zing from his touch, she held up the list. "You've already done a lot."

"I don't want you overworked." He shoved his hands into the pockets of his slacks. "I've hired a DJ for the engagement party. We're going to show up C. J. and Cicely on the dance floor."

Summer got to her feet, pleased her knees were rock-steady, and rounded the desk. "You and C. J. are always competing against each other."

Sin chuckled. "I don't want to let him get a big head."

"He'd probably say the same thing about you."

"I imagine he would," Sin mused.

She reached for a card on her desk and gave it to him. "The name of the caterer that Mrs. Callahan swears by and the list of food I serve. She can call me if she has any questions. The Yankees are playing the weekend of your party."

Shaking his head, Sin took the card and slipped it into the pocket of his jacket. "With all you have going on, you still thought of me."

I'm always thinking of you. "You needed the information. I don't want your reputation to suffer."

"Summer." He whispered her name in that deep, wanton voice of his, and her skin prickled with pleasure.

She knew the hug was coming and was unable to avoid it. His strong arms pulled her against the disturbing warmth of his muscular body, enfolding her in temptation and endless possibilities. She felt her heart race, hoped he didn't feel it as well.

He set her away and stared down at her with the most beguiling black eyes she'd ever seen. "If you can make it to my place around eight thirty, I'll have breakfast—crepes or omelets that I promise not to cook. Afterward you can look the place over."

Her heart tried to settle into a normal rhythm. "Crepes with blueberries."

"See you then." He went to the door. "You look tempting in that dress."

The door closed, and Summer eased back against the desk. "Sin, what are you doing to me?"

Sin found himself grinning like a kid at his first baseball game as he tried not to hover too much over his housekeeper, Lynne, while she cooked breakfast the next morning in his kitchen. In her midsixties, tall, slender, scrupulously neat, she had a passion for her two grandchildren, baseball, and chocolate—in that order. The previous owners of the penthouse had recommended her. He'd liked the plainspoken woman instantly, and she kept the two-story place spotless.

He glanced at the bone-china place settings on the footed, hand-carved mahogany island with seating for four, the long-stemmed gladiolas in the crystal vase. He wanted everything to be perfect. He'd gone out early that morning and purchased the flowers. Summer loved flowers.

The doorbell rang. "Go answer that. By the time you get back, I'll have everything on the serving dishes, and I'll make myself scarce and start clean-ing upstairs."

Sin stopped in midstride. "Lynne, you don't have to do that. Summer is just a friend. She's coming to look the place over for the party."

Lynne slid the crepe into a chafing dish before turning to him. "She's the first woman you've in-vited here, as far as I know. She's definitely the first I've cooked for, so you won't send the poor thing to the hospital. You could have just had coffee. I al-ways set the pot on automatic before I leave."

"Summer's not a coffee drinker. Besides, she works hard at her restaurant seeing that others are well fed; she deserves someone to see about her," he explained to his housekeeper for what seemed the fifteenth time since he'd told her yesterday that he'd have a guest for breakfast. "She's going to be busy in the coming weeks. She's done a lot for me. I just wanted to do something nice for her."

Lynne put a hand on her nonexistent hip. "You know I like coming in after nine so I can cook for my daughter and grandchildren before they leave for work and school. You never asked me to come in early before."

"Lynne."

The doorbell chimed again. Lynne went to the refrigerator. "Go let her in."

He frowned at his housekeeper's back and felt compelled to say, "She's just a friend."

"A beautiful one, if the picture on your desk in your office is any indication."

"So what?" he said, his cheerful mood evaporating. He'd taken the picture of Summer the evening before she left for Paris. Her aunt and uncle had given her a going-away party. Afterward they had all taken a walk on the beach behind their house. Summer had sat on the sand, the rushes in the background, her knees upraised with her arms around them, laughing at a neighbor's poodle trying to catch a turtle.

The doorbell chime came again.

Sin headed for the door. What was with Lynne? Just like a woman to get an idiotic notion into her head and not let it go. He jerked open the door to find Summer standing there with her hand upraised. Slowly she lowered it.

"We can go for a walk. I'm not very hungry."

She was doing it again. Giving unselfishly. "Come on in, breakfast is getting cold."

After a long moment, she came inside. "I don't mind coming back."

The past couple of times Summer had been to his place, she had always commented on the magnificent view of Central Park through the two-story wall of glass, the lovely sweep of the black-wrought-iron staircase with a mahogany railing leading to the second floor, the French silk–covered walls, the Venetian chandelier hanging over the entry table.

Now her entire attention was focused on him. Now she just wanted to comfort him.

What man worth anything wouldn't want to make such a caring woman's life a little better? He just liked making her happy. The turmoil in him eased. His hands settled on her shoulders, felt the slight trembling beneath. Something inside him twisted. He'd done that to her. He'd caused her to worry unnecessarily.

"I'm fine, and we're eating breakfast. An annoying conversation before you arrived is the reason I'm out of sorts. Your crepes are ready." He took her arm. "After breakfast, we can look the place over."

Entering the kitchen, he found that Lynne wasn't there. Apparently she had taken the back stairs in the kitchen to the second floor. The previous owner loved to cook so the area was immense, with French period cabinetry with curves, intricate marquerterie, and a rich, antique finish. All of the doors were embellished with intricately inlaid veneer patterns. Sand-burned medallion designs were surrounded with book- and mirror-matched burl. "Please have a seat."

Summer paused and glanced around the large kitchen. "Magnificent. I could live in here."

Sin didn't understand why Summer's statement made him restless. Picking up the pitcher of orange juice, he filled her glass. Ice clinked against the sides. "Until you had to trade your mattress for Italian marble."

She grinned. "Might be worth it. Come sit down. I'm hungrier than I thought, and these crepes look delicious and freshly made." She served both of them. "Do you have a genie I don't know about?"

Sin sat on the padded leather chair beside her. "Lynne, my housekeeper."

Summer said grace then lifted her head and reached for her fork to take a bite. "Delicious. One question."

Pretty sure it would be to ask if she could come over again for breakfast, he reached for his fork. "Shoot."

"Why isn't she cooking breakfast for you every day?"

Sin's fork hovered over his crepe, then he raised

his head. He might have known. Lowering his head, he said, "She likes to come in later."

Silence ensued, then he felt her hand, small and capable, on his arm. "Thank you." She picked back up her fork. "One thing we won't have to worry about is the staff bumping into one another. There's enough room in the kitchen. Excuse me."

"Where are you going?" Sin asked, sliding off the chair.

"Checking the refrigerator." Summer opened it, then shook her head. "I see the ingredients to make our breakfast, but not much else."

"It's easier eating out," he explained, fighting the urge to squirm.

Closing the door, she gracefully retook her seat. "We're going to need that room, so don't change habits and fill it up."

"Not likely." He picked up his fork. "Any idea of how to get the wow?"

Summer smiled. "Just walking though the door with the sun going down over Central Park will do it for most, but for the others I have a few ideas. First, I want to take a tour. Then we can go online and check out Elegant Decor Events."

"Elegant Decor Events?"

"Yes, the best rental company in New York."

Chapter 6

"Sin, not to hurt your feelings, but there isn't much you could contribute to my meeting with Krystal," Summer told him later that morning in her office.

She'd mentioned the meeting with Krystal when she was leaving his penthouse. He'd insisted on joining them. She'd told him that wasn't necessary and left. Five minutes before the appointment time with Krystal, he knocked on her office door. In typical Sin fashion, he'd ignored her wishes.

Sitting across from Summer with one leg crossed over his knee, Sin didn't look up from entering information on his iPhone. "I'm staying. Especially after seeing Elegant Decor Events' Web site. I never knew so much went into planning a party."

"That might have been an error in judgment," Summer admitted ruefully.

There was a knock on her door. Sin stood and opened the door. Krystal came in, followed by Alex and Dianne. Surprised, Summer rounded her desk. Alex had on a beautiful black pin-striped suit while Dianne wore a black sheath with gold clunky jewelry.

"Hi, everyone," Summer greeted. "I expected Krystal, but what are you two doing here?" The words were barely out before she stared at Sin. "Or should I ask?"

"As best man, it's my job to ensure everything that involves the groom goes off flawlessly." He waved Dianne and Krystal to seats in front of the desk. "Let's not waste time since we all have to get back to work. Krystal, you're up first."

"First, thanks to all of you for wanting to help." The attractive young woman in her early thirties was dressed comfortably in faded jeans and a Callahan's black tee with gold letters. She swallowed and perched on the edge of the seat.

"Thank you for wanting to do this for C. J. and Cicely." Dianne took a seat and glanced up at Alex standing beside her. Love radiated from her. "We personally know how important this is."

Alex stared down at Dianne, smoothed the back of his hand over her cheek. "It will finally start to be real for them—knowing how blessed and lucky they are that their heart's desire will be with them forever."

Summer braced her hands on top of her desk and leaned back. Alex, usually the quiet one of the three friends, adored his bride and said so at every opportunity. Would she ever come close to knowing what it felt like to be loved that way by a man?

"Focus, you two," Sin told them. "Krystal."

Probably not, Summer thought, and did what Sin said, focused on the situation at hand, not her unruly feelings that would never be voiced.

Moistening her lips, Krystal took a folded sheet of notebook paper out of her purse, looked up, swallowed again. "I'm not much on decorating."

"Neither am I, but we have Summer and Dianne to help," Sin said with confidence.

Alex said, "Whatever you have, I'm sure it's fine."

Summer applauded the way the men were treating Krystal. Krystal, on the other hand, kept looking at Sin and Alex as if she couldn't take her eyes off them. Dianne, apparently used to the appreciative stares her husband received, didn't seem bothered.

"I believe you mentioned streamers and balloons," Summer prompted to get the other woman going. This was no time to be thinking of jumping Sin.

The woman's gaze guilty jumped back to Summer. "Yes, pink-and-white streamers and balloons." She glanced down at the paper in her hand, then back up. "We can order a sheet cake. You know about the hamburger sliders and onion rings. That's all I have."

Complete silence.

Again Krystal moistened her lips—painted a racy red—and glanced around at everyone in the room. "If it's not right, please say something. You wouldn't let a person walk in front of a speeding bus, would you?"

Sin walked over to stand beside Summer. "I don't think C. J. is a pink-and-white kind of guy."

"Balloons definitely played a role in their relationship, so that's good," Alex put in.

"Definitely," Dianne added.

Sin looked at Summer. "Other thoughts on a theme? Color scheme?"

Summer slowly looked at Sin. If Krystal hadn't looked so distressed and hopeful, she would have given him a sharp jab. So now *he* was the expert. "Krystal, you have a great beginning. I think we just need to embellish it a bit. How about we use petal pink and add moss green and olive to your choice? The pink can be for romance, the green the birth of their love, the new beginning of their lives together."

"Perfect." Dianne turned in her seat to Krystal. "Instead of crepe paper for the streamers, I know I can find beautiful satin ribbon in those colors, maybe three inches wide. We can use inch-wide ribbon to hang from the balloons we place at the top of each streamer arch."

"Sin can be in charge of blowing up the balloons," Summer said with a straight face. *Payback time.*

He didn't blink. "Isn't it a good thing that I know where to rent a helium tank?"

Her lips twitched. "Isn't it."

"Table setting. Mother always said that was important." Alex smiled down at Dianne. "My beautiful wife said the same thing at our first dinner party."

"You have smart women in your life, Alex, and you're smart to remember what they said." Summer rounded her desk, stooped, and placed a pilsner glass with an arrangement of greenery and white roses and a shot glass with a white votive on the table.

Dianne and Krystal sighed.

"We should have things that represent something they love," Summer said.

"I can get miniature wrought-iron mannequin dress forms and thread with the same ribbon as the streamers," Dianna suggested. "We could have one at the sign-in table on the bar. Large pillar candles tied with the ribbon would also look nice."

"We can keep the roses or go with blue and green hydrangeas. What do you think?" Summer asked the group.

"C. J. sent Cicely white roses when she was in Paris," Alex said.

"White roses it is, then." Sin glanced at Summer. "Do you think we could have a special floral arrangement in a miniature dress form made for Cicely to take home?"

Summer stared at him. "What?"

"That party site you had me look at mentioned guests taking home mementos. I thought it would be a good idea for Cicely to have something."

"That's a lovely idea, Sin." Dianne sighed. "I have

keepsakes from after we were engaged, but I wish I had things from the time we were dating."

"You have me." Alex leaned over and brushed his lips across his wife's.

Sin grunted. "You two are pitiful. It's a good thing I love both of you."

Alex chuckled. "Likewise."

Summer didn't want to think about how her body clenched when Sin mentioned love. She'd definitely better get a grip.

"Oh," Krystal said, her eyes blinking rapidly. "I can see it. It's going to be beautiful. The Boss and Cicely will be able to hold their heads up and remember the night with a smile."

"You had the original idea," Summer told her.

"We all know it was a far cry from what it is now. I have friends who are willing to help with making whatever food you planned," Krystal went on to say. "I know you're busy with your restaurant. You just tell me when and where to have them."

"Count me in to help." Dianne came to her feet.

"Thanks, but I've already spoken to a couple of my staff members, who are more than happy to earn the extra money." Summer straightened. "Krystal, there are a few things I need to ask you to consider changing."

"Whatever." Krystal lifted both hands palms-out. "It's as good as done."

Summer nodded. "The bar will probably be crowded. Desserts, just like the food, need to be small so the guests can eat them in a couple of bites, not try to balance a plate with perhaps a drink. How about yellow mini cupcakes with piped pink roses, and chocolate cupcakes with a chocolate glaze and their names written in white buttercream icing? I think really small white plates—which the bar has—and moss-green linen napkins will add a touch of pizzazz and casual elegance."

Krystal came to her feet and went to Summer. "I'm not giving up that somewhere out there is a man who won't cheat on me. If I find him, will you help me plan things?"

Summer was touched and reminded that she didn't give up, either. She wouldn't force the issue with Sin, but if the opportunity presented itself, she was taking it. "Since you had the original idea, why don't we help each other?"

"Deal." Krystal stepped back. "My cousin works at a bakery, I'll call her on the way back about the cupcakes. There's a florist near the bar. If you'll get me the ribbon, me and the girls will make the streamers and the guys can hang them."

"I'll bring the ribbon by this afternoon and look for balloons in the same shades. Pick up the pillar candles," Dianne told her.

"Drop a swatch of the ribbon by here and I'll find the napkins." Summer reached for her notebook. "I can't wait to see how this comes together."

"Me either." Krystal hitched up the wide strap of her purse on her shoulder. "I better be going."

"We're right behind you," Alex said, taking Dianne's arm. "Coming, Sin?"

"In a minute," he said.

"What?" Summer asked once they were alone. "And since, as you said, we all have to get to work, please don't drag this out."

"You said you weren't interested in anyone."

"Pardon?"

"If you aren't interested in anyone, what was that talk about helping plan things with Krystal?"

Summer rolled her eyes and took a seat behind her desk. "You and C. J. are a pair."

"So, did you find someone?" And if she had, why did the thought bother him?

"And when between our meeting Monday and today would I have had the time?"

"It can happen suddenly, I'm told," Sin said.

Summer leaned back in her chair. If she thought he was jealous, she'd do a happy dance. He wasn't. "If and when that times comes, I plan to keep him a secret until we're engaged. Otherwise, you and C. J. would scare him off."

"If we could scare him off, he wouldn't be worth keeping," he said.

"Good point." She picked up her pen. "Now get lost."

For some odd reason, he wasn't ready to leave. Summer was no pushover, but some guys ran a good game. No guy was going to mistreat her the way some idiot had Krystal.

"Bye, Sin."

If he told her what he was thinking, she'd boot him out the door. "There's another reason I wanted to get more of a handle on my party, and C. J. and Cicely's party finalized," Sin said. "I'll be busy for the next three or four days. There's sports events all weekend, then I'm flying out to my Phoenix office Monday afternoon. The All-Star game is there Tuesday, then the next day I'm flying to LA to visit my office and the ESPY Awards that night."

"Well, isn't it a good thing you have a private jet?"

Sin twisted his head to one side. She wasn't the sarcastic type. "If you need me, call. We can go to the Elegant Decor Events warehouse when I come back, then I'm all yours."

Summer ducked her head and began shuffling folders on her desk. "Great. Have a safe trip."

He stared at her. Something wasn't right, but he couldn't put his finger on it.

"If you can come by my place in the morning for a taste test to get the food finalized, it would be great." She folded her slim hands on her desk.

"I'll skip breakfast." Whatever it was bothering her seemed to have passed.

She wrinkled her nose. "You mean your bagel and coffee if you don't have a business meeting. I saw inside your refrigerator."

"Like I said. It's easier eating out."

Summer frowned. He needed someone to take

care of him. She pulled her thoughts back. "I'll see you in the morning around ten."

"I'll be there. We'll make an awesome pair."

"Yes." *Just not romantically.*

Sin's cell phone rang. He looked at the readout, then put it away. He didn't have anything to say to Glen Atkins. The man was an egocentric, arrogant pain in the rear. Sin wasn't looking forward to seeing him at the ESPY Awards next week.

"Someone you didn't want to talk with?" she asked, finally meeting and holding his gaze.

"Yeah. One of my clients who is tossing away his career with both hands," Sin told Summer, still trying to figure out what was going on with her. It wasn't the sadness he'd glimpsed at the party, but he couldn't figure out exactly what. And asking her wouldn't get him anywhere. "Unfortunately, some people don't realize that they only get one shot in life."

She frowned. "He won't listen to you?"

"Or anyone else. He thinks he is indispensable."

"No one is indispensable."

He stared at her a long time. Successful, beautiful, and she would do anything for those she loved. "I wouldn't be so sure about that. Bye, Summer."

The next morning, relaxing on a padded stool at the counter in Summer's bright blue-and-white kitchen, Sin felt completely at ease. Her kitchen was nothing like his, and it pleased him immensely. Hers might not have the custom cabinetry or the space, but it felt homier, warmer. Or perhaps the woman at the stove humming softly made it that way.

He liked watching her bustle around the kitchen. The sight brought back warm memories of her coaxing him into tasting one of her experimental dishes before and after she'd gone to Paris. She'd always been serious about her cooking, and about the path she wanted to take to honor her parents' dream while forging her own.

She'd done both.

Folding his arm, Sin wondered if he should tell her she looked kind of cute in her frilly blue apron tied around a slim-fitting teal dress. Nope. Not if he didn't want to be beaned with the wooden spoon in her hand.

Scooping up the Mexican rice she'd been stirring, Summer walked over to where he sat. "Tell me what you think?"

Without hesitation he accepted the offering. "Delicious, but I knew it would be. But you're not cooking that night, are you?"

"No way." She opened an earthenware dish for a soft tortilla, then placed sizzling chicken strips grilled with onions, red peppers, and green peppers on top and added pico de gallo, shredded cheese, lettuce, and tomatoes. Placing the fajita on a plate, she handed it to him. "I'll marinate the meat beforehand. Once at your place, my guys will cook the food for the buffet tables."

He made no attempt to eat. "How much prep work are you doing for this party?"

Summer wasn't as surprised by the question as she was that Sin wasn't eating. He loved food. "Not much."

He sat the blue-and-white plate on the counter. "Hire more people if you have to. You're doing enough already."

He was being protective again. She shouldn't wish it was more. "I can handle this." She picked up the plate and held out a fork. "Eat."

He picked up the fajita, his gaze on her, and lifted it to her mouth. "You first. I'm not a breakfast person, but you are, and I bet you haven't eaten."

She hadn't. She bit into the tortilla. "Good."

He took a generous bite and nodded his agreement. Summer didn't know why her stomach got that free-falling sensation seeing him place his mouth where hers had been.

Afraid he'd see the flush on her face, she went to the refrigerator. Hopefully the cool air and the flan would help. "Now try this."

His gaze flickered to the glistening dessert in a ramekin dish with a brown glazed crust as he polished off his food. "I told you I don't like flan when we talked about the menu. Too much like pudding."

She picked up a spoon. "And I told you, you have to please your guests. Open."

"No." He primped his lips.

She laughed at his lips pressed together. "Sin, don't be such a baby. Just taste it."

He shook his head. Still laughing, she stepped into the V of his legs without thinking to get closer and touched the spoon to his mouth.

"Yuc—"

She took the opportunity to feed him the spoonful. She didn't realize the precarious position she was in until his hands bracketed her waist. She started to step back. His hands stopped her. She felt trapped by the sensual pull of his body, the sudden narrowing of his midnight-black eyes; then it was gone.

"How would you like me to force-feed something you detested?"

"I like most foods," she said, hoping that her voice sounded normal instead of bordering on arousal, that he didn't notice her hands shaking.

"Smarty." He took the spoon and dish from her hand and took another bite. "What else are you going to feed me?"

"Guacamole dip." She hurried away and returned with the tray and chips.

Sin just sat there.

"You didn't mention you don't like guacamole."

"That's because I do."

"Well." She inched the dish closer.

Sin grinned slow and easy. "Aren't you going to come closer and feed it to me?"

The thought had her hands trembling the tiniest bit. Sin was teasing her again. She placed the tray on the counter by his arm. "Not when you have two good hands. And when we finish, you get to help with dishes."

He munched on a chip. "You sure know how to dampen a guy's mood."

Summer busied herself at the stove. If only she could do the same for herself.

Emerging from the cab in front of his office building later that morning, Sin was smiling. The tasting and teasing had been fun. With her culinary skills Summer had once again proven him wrong about not liking a certain food. He should have expected as much. She was in a class by herself.

"Mr. Sinclair."

Hearing his name, Sin paused and turned. Seeing Marsha Williams, he wished he hadn't. The great beginning of his day with Summer took a nosedive. He wasn't looking forward to the coming conversation with Marsha, but perhaps it was time the woman eagerly rushing toward him faced reality. He certainly had to.

He knew what she wanted, knew what it was to wish things were different. However, just as in his own life, when he had to accept the hard truth, Marsha would have to do the same.

She stopped in front of him and bit her lower lip. She was a small woman, barely five foot three. With her shoulders briefly hunched, she looked even smaller, fragile. "I need to talk to you."

Silently Sin took her arm and entered his office building, assisting her through security. Neither spoke on the elevator ride to his floor. Opening the door to his outer office, he greeted his secretary, noted the surprise on her face. Marsha Williams had been on the television and in the tabloids. This wasn't the first time she had tried to speak with him. She'd never gotten past security downstairs.

"Mrs. Douglas, please hold my calls."

"Yes, sir."

Opening his office door, Sin waved Marsha to a chair in front of his desk and took his seat. "I'm sorry, but this will have to be quick. I have an appointment in ten minutes."

She swallowed, brushed her hand over her stylishly auburn cut hair. She was wearing a white sundress and was an attractive young woman in her midtwenties, with desperate eyes. "Glen won't take my calls. I thought you could talk to him." She swallowed, fought tears. "I need to talk to him about the baby."

Sin's hands flexed on his desk. In his career, he'd seen countless women take drastic measures to meet athletes. They all thought they would be different from all of the other women before them. He'd yet to see it work out that way. "I'm sorry, Ms. Williams. There's nothing I can do."

"Please." She came to her feet, her hand clutching

her stomach. "My parents made me get the lawyer. I didn't want to bring the paternity suit. If I could just talk to Glen, we'd fix this. I know he loves me."

Glen loved himself, first, last, and always. Yet Sin couldn't bring himself to tell the vulnerable young woman before him. She looked at the breaking point. "I'm sorry."

"Stop saying that," she shouted. "My baby needs a father. I need Glen."

"Glen Atkins is the last thing you need," Sin said calmly, although his temper was boiling. Marsha wasn't the usual groupie that hung around athletes hoping to get "lucky" or "paid." She was a nice woman from a good family. She actually believed Glen loved her. "What you need is a man who'll stand by you, not someone who only thinks of himself. Your baby does need a father, but a father is more than a sperm donor."

Her eyes widened in anger. She stepped back. "You don't know anything. Maybe you're the kind of man who would turn his back on his child; Glen wouldn't do that." She brushed the tears away from her eyes. "If you won't help me, I'll find someone who will." Turning, she left, closing the door behind her.

Sin leaned back in his chair. She was wrong on so many counts—about him, about the type of man Glen Atkins was.

Glen liked easy women, good times, his huge ego stroked. His celebrity status drew women, and he used that ruthlessly. Most of the women were as worthless and as shallow as he was. They'd bail at the first bump.

Sin thought of one woman who would be there no matter what. *Summer.* She'd go the distance for those she loved. She'd proven that over and over. What's more, unlike the impressionable Marsha Williams, Summer would have instantly seen through Glen's lies and sent him on his way.

But one day a man without lies or deceit would come into her life, and she'd fall in love and get married, have children. An unexpected sense of loss swamped Sin. He rubbed his chest at the tightness he felt, shook his head, then reached for his day calendar.

His protective instincts were kicking in again, that was all. His housekeeper was way off base. Summer and he were friends. Just friends.

Chapter 7

"Summer, thank you for letting us meet in your office." Cicely sat on the small sofa in Summer's office Wednesday night. Dianne was next to her.

"You're more than welcome," Summer told her. She'd pulled a chair from in front of her desk to join them.

"Dianne, thank you for coming," Cicely said. "Ladies, this time the chocolate and wine are on me."

"Mighty good wine." Dianne lifted her glass. "My compliments to you and Summer's excellent wine cellar."

"Excellent chocolate." Summer popped an imported Swiss truffle into her mouth. Because she was at work, she had declined the wine. She could have used a glass. She really missed Sin. The rat hadn't called since he left.

Cicely took a deep breath and briefly grabbed both of their hands. "I can't put this off any longer. I know we haven't known each other a long time, but each of you has enriched my life so much. Without your help, I wouldn't be marrying the man of my heart. You helped us get together."

"I think you did that yourself," Summer said, a mischievous smile on her lips, glad she hadn't experienced even one jealous twinge since she had begun working with Sin on his party.

Dianne nodded in agreement. "Alex said C. J. was a goner the moment he saw you at Callahan's."

"And fought it." Cicely twisted her wineglass in her hand. "I did as well."

"And now you're getting married next June." Dianne sighed softly.

"I don't know how we'll get it all done by then, but there's one thing I have to do tonight." Cicely placed her wineglass on the table in front of her, then took the hands of the two women. "Both of you mean so much to me, so the only way I could do this was to put both of your names in a hat and let C. J. draw."

Summer felt a twinge of regret. Before this moment she had been feeling a bit out of sorts to be asked to be a bridesmaid—for the tenth time. Now, realizing that she might not even be in the wedding, she was disappointed.

"Summer, would you please be my maid of honor?"

Stunned, Summer stared at Cicely. Moments ticked by.

Cicely shifted uncomfortably in her seat. "If you want. I mean—"

Squealing, Summer rushed over and hugged Cicely. "Thank you. I'm honored. However, I have to admit I've been a bridesmaid, but never a maid of honor."

"You're sure?" Cicely asked, a tiny frown wrinkling her brow.

Summer didn't take offense. After all, she had told Cicely and C. J. she was jealous of them. Cicely having her as her maid of honor was an honor she hadn't expected. "Positive. I thought you were going to say you didn't have room for one of us in your wedding party. I was disappointed, and sitting here hoping I'd be gracious about losing."

Dianne chuckled. "I was thinking the same thing."

"No." Cicely shook her head. "Dianne, I want you to be one of my bridesmaids."

"Done," Dianne said.

Summer pressed her hand to her chest. "A maid of honor. Wow! Thank you."

"You might not thank me later." Cicely held up a printout. "You have to keep me on schedule, ensure things are going smoothly. My assistant saw my list on my desk yesterday and put everything into my calendar and made me triplicates, put it on two flash drives. One for home and for the office. I admit, I'm most anxious about the gown." She looked at Dianne. "Yours was gorgeous and exactly you. Beautiful and alluring with a hint of sexiness."

Dianne smiled. "I almost drove Greg, our designer, crazy while he was helping me design the gown, but it was exactly what I wanted."

"You were beautiful. Alex couldn't take his eyes off you," Cicely said, her expression wistful.

"Nor I him, and you and C. J. will be the same way."

Summer looked at them, the secret smiles, and playfully punched both of their shoulders. "No fair."

"One day you'll know and feel what we feel," Cicely predicted.

Dianne didn't say anything, but Summer felt her eyes on her. Sin was a friend. He'd made that clear. She just had to get her heart to accept it. "Far into the future. Now, where is that list?"

"Here." Cicely handed Summer a flash drive and the printed list. "I made you a copy of both."

Summer accepted them with a grateful smile. "I won't let you down."

"Neither will I," Dianne said.

Cicely blinked, then leaned forward to place an arm around each woman's shoulder. "Thank you. My—my family's not happy with me, but I love C. J. too much to care."

"My parents disowned me when I wouldn't bow to their wishes," Dianne reminded her. "Alex makes up for it and so much more."

"We're your family now." Summer's arms tightened. "We're here for you."

"Damn straight, and if you forget it we'll steer

you toward the ugliest wedding dress in the universe," Dianne promised, a catch in her voice.

Cicely laughed, straightened, wiped away a tear. "It feels good to have friends, good friends."

"Yes," Dianne and Summer said in unison.

"I guess that's all." Cicely rose to her feet and so did the other women.

"I'll walk out with you." Summer placed the flash drive and printed list on her desk.

Dianne opened the office door. "Alex and C. J. are at the bar watching the ESPYs on ESPN."

"Do you think we'll see Sin?" Cicely asked as they walked though the restaurant.

Summer couldn't help the little leap of her heart. "He was interviewed last year when several of his clients won awards."

"Looks like Sin has camera time again, but he's not smiling." Dianne nodded toward one of the three flat-screens TVs in the bar.

Summer saw the hard frown on Sin's face as he stood beside an attractive brunette in a low-cut, strapless red gown. She kept blinking as if the bright lights of the cameras bothered her eyes.

"He said he wasn't seeing anyone," Summer murmured, wondering how she could speak when jealousy almost choked her, and her heart had a huge hole in it.

"You know Sin is as truthful as they come," Alex said, standing when the women stopped behind him and C. J. "Must be another reason."

C. J. came off his stool as well. "Yeah, you'd be surprised at the way women throw themselves at men. Last year—"

Summer saw Alex elbow C. J., and wondered if Cicely had seen the exchange. Summer didn't have to wait long to have her answer.

"Please go on," Cicely said sweetly.

C. J. jerked his startled gaze to Alex, who now had his arm around his wife and his attention to the TV screen again. Clearly he didn't plan to get into the same trouble C. J. found himself in.

"I—er . . . That was long ago and forgotten," C. J. said, trying to pull Cicely closer.

She put her hands on his chest to stop him. "Explain."

Since she wouldn't come closer, C. J. leaned his forehead against hers. "I fell in love with an incredible woman who loves me almost as much. I told Sin when he asked me about the All-Star game and the ESPYs that he could give my tickets away. I had something better to do. Be with the woman I love."

Cicely's arms curved around his neck. "You were wrong. I love you just as much."

"Honey." He tenderly kissed her on the forehead, pulled her closer. "We're going home."

Makeup sex time, Summer thought and glanced back at the TV screen. They were interviewing Ron Washington, the head coach of the Texas Rangers and the coach of the American League for the All-

Star game. Sin was out of camera range, and so was the woman.

The question that drummed in Summer's brain was: Where had they gone?

Sin needed to get out of LA. Since things were going well in his LA office there was no reason for him to stay. He'd called his pilot the moment he'd seen Marsha back to her hotel where her anxious mother waited for her.

Marsha had convinced her mother that she needed to get away for a few days. The woman had no idea what her daughter had planned. It had blown up in her face. Glen had been deliberately cruel, and so had the sneering woman with him.

Sin had been too late to do anything but help Marsha to his car. An alert cameraman had caught them and, of course, expected a lover's quarrel. She was devastated, but hopefully she was finally convinced that the man she thought loved her was a heartless braggart.

As soon as the jet was airborne and he was cleared to use his phone, he called Summer. He wasn't sure why he felt so melancholy. Perhaps because neither Michael, Alex, nor C. J. was with him. Or just the fact that, once again, he'd seen that love caused pain.

"Radcliffe's."

Closing his eyes, Sin leaned his head back against the leather seat. "I just wanted to hear your voice." He sat up. He hadn't meant to say that.

"What about the woman I saw you with on television at the EPSYs? She's unavailable?"

"I thought you knew me better," he said, feeling old beyond his years.

"Sin—"

"She was in trouble. The man she thought loved her had just humiliated her in front of his new plaything and his entourage." Unbuckling his seat belt, he came to his feet. "She's carrying his child and the bastard couldn't care less."

"I'm sorry. She must be devastated."

"Yeah." Sin rubbed his hand over his head. Life sucked at times.

"If she has you in her corner, despite the situation, she's lucky. I should know."

"You didn't think so a moment ago."

"Long night."

He was instantly alert. "What happened?"

"Cicely asked me to be her maid of honor."

"You aren't pleased?"

"Immensely. I'll let you in on a little secret. I was jealous of all the happiness going on around us. That's what was wrong with me at the engagement party at Aunt Evelyn's house. Tell me how horrible I am."

He took his seat. He didn't have to think long to know the reason she was telling him now. She was trying to take his mind off whatever was bothering him. That by doing so she exposed herself didn't matter. "You're human. We're going to make a good team."

There was a slight pause. "Always have. Always will."

He frowned. Her voice didn't sound right. He wished he could see her face. "How about I pick you up in the morning around eight thirty, we grab a bite, and we go browse Elegant Decor Events?"

"Sounds like a plan. And Sin?"

"Yeah?"

"No matter what, we'll always be friends."

"Always have. Always will."

"Safe travel. Bye."

Sin held the phone and wondered why, for the first time, talking to Summer hadn't centered him, made things better. Instead, he was more restless than ever.

The next morning Summer's legs pumped as she raced on her exercise bike, but no matter how fast she pedaled, she couldn't go fast enough to outrun the images of her and Sin. His fingers stroked her cheeks then slid into her unbound hair. His mouth, hot and sure, lowered to hers, nibbling on her lower lip before his tongue lazily swirled against hers, driving her crazy and making her whimper with need before moving to the curve of her neck, then lower to the swell of her breast. Her breath hitched over her lips as his mouth opened to take the aching nipple—

The ringing of the doorbell made her jump guiltily. Her gaze swung to the clock on the wall. Eight thirty-two. *Sin.*

Summer shut her eyes. She'd been so caught up in her fantasy about him, she'd lost track of time. She wanted him. No matter how she tried to fight it, the need grew.

And she was tired of fighting it. But never again would she be jealous and snippy with him. Like Alex said, Sin didn't lie. She knew that in her head, but she'd spoken from her hurting heart.

The chime sounded again. She came off the bike, grabbed a towel to blot her face, and headed out of the second bedroom she'd turned into an exercise room. She opened the door, hoping Sin couldn't tell that the flush on her face wasn't entirely due to exercise. "Hi. Sorry."

His gaze tracked her from her hair in a knot on the top of her head, over the sweaty tank clinging to her breasts, to her shorts. "Hi. Don't worry. I know how it is when you're getting a good burn."

Burn was right, but not the one he was referring to. "Come on in. I'll take a quick shower and be out in ten."

He stepped inside, studying her closely. "You all right? Last night you sounded . . ." He shrugged. "Different."

She barely kept from flushing guiltily. "My bad manners in accusing you. I'm sorry about that as well."

"Forget it. You better get that shower." Shoving his hands into his pockets, he headed for the kitchen. "I'll take juice since you don't have coffee."

Puzzled, Summer stared after him. She would have said she knew Sin in all of his moods. This morning he seemed to be a bit on edge, restless. She'd never seen him that way.

"Hurry if we're going to get breakfast," he said as he kept walking.

Summer spun toward the bedroom, closing the door behind her, undressing as she crossed the bedroom and headed for the shower. She usually liked to soak in the tub when she finished exercising, but this morning there wasn't time. Naked, she stepped under the shower spray and tried to push from her mind that Sin was only a short distance away, that she wished he was with her.

Sin sipped the orange juice he didn't want. He needed something to cool him off and get his mind off the way the damp T-shirt clung to Summer's high, firm breasts, the tempting impression of her nipple. He'd wanted to . . .

He gulped another drink. He didn't lust after his women friends.

He scowled. If he wasn't such a lousy housekeeper and thought he could find someone as good as Lynne, he'd fire her. This was her fault for messing up his mind.

Like Summer had said last night, they would

always be friends. Friends didn't want to get each other naked more than their next breath.

"Ready."

He whirled around, and attributed the sudden increase in his heart rate to her startling him. It couldn't have been the way the red knit fabric hugged her breasts, her elegantly shaped body. "Let me rinse this."

Summer chuckled. "A domesticated Sin. I can't believe it."

"Believe it." Setting the rinsed glass in the sink, he turned to see her contorting her arms trying to reach behind her back.

"What is it?"

Blowing out a breath, she let her hands fall to her sides. "The zipper. I love this dress, but trying to zip it up and not take a chunk out of my hair when it's down is always iffy. I was hurrying and forgot to pin it up." She turned her back to him and lifted her hair out of the way. "Do you mind?"

He went to her, caught the scent of lavender and jasmine. His hands trembled.

"Is my hair in the way?"

"No," he said, his voice sounding rough to his ears. *Just do it*. He grasped the zipper and tugged upward, his fingers brushing against her soft, flawless skin. He wanted to lean closer, to press—

"Got it?"

Sin jumped. What the hell! He quickly stepped back. "Done." He headed for the door. He didn't know what was happening here, but it stopped now.

Summer made it through breakfast and their visit to Elegant Decor Events through sheer determination. Hours later, she could still feel the light brush of Sin's knuckles against her skin.

"You're a wicked woman," she murmured to herself as she frosted the last cake. And she was paying for it. Her skin felt overly sensitive. She could have gone to her bedroom and pinned up her hair, but she'd thought it might be sexy for him to do it for her. What it was, was crazy, especially after she had made such a big deal of them being friends.

Finished, she placed the glass dome over the frosted cake and took her supplies to the sink, where she caught bits of conversation of Joan and Karen, another waitress, talking about their dates last night. Apparently, sex was had by all.

"You all right, Summer?"

"What?" Summer glanced up to see Joan and Karen staring at her.

"You've been washing that same pan for the past five minutes," Joan explained, her eyes narrowed.

Summer jerked her gaze back to the sink. She had an excellent dishwasher, but she always liked to hand-wash her cake pans. She'd brought them with her from Paris. "Just thinking."

Joan edged to one side of Summer, Karen to the other. "About the party?" Joan asked.

Summer grabbed the out Joan had given her. "Sin has very specific ideas as to what he wants."

Karen giggled. "I have definite ideas about what I want to do to Sin."

"Me, too," Joan agreed with a wicked grin. "He's always polite, and definitely not interested. Not even the girls can entice him."

Summer was glad she was looking down at the last pan while the two women were discussing Sin. She glanced at Joan's "girls" then down at her own breasts. No comparison to Joan's BBB.

Joan picked up a drying cloth and a pan. "That's one mouthwatering man."

Karen put away the dried cake pan. "My knees shake when I see him."

"But you're dating other men," Summer blurted.

Joan and Karen looked at each other and burst out laughing. Karen went on to explain, "We're having fun. We're young. But with Sin, I would be all his."

"In a heartbeat." The women slapped hands.

Summer knew just how they felt. "Thank you for helping." Removing her apron, she hung it up on a peg and went to her office. With all the women wanting Sin, she didn't stand a chance.

Sin wasn't a coward. Plus, he wasn't going to shirk his responsibility as best man.

Tonight was C. J. and Cicely's engagement party. He'd avoided being around Summer as long as he could. If he knew Summer, and he did, she was probably doing the lion's share of work for the party. She'd need his help.

He discovered he was right when he looked though the window in the swinging kitchen door and saw her fastening a plastic top on a sandwich tray. He counted five trays.

He rapped on the window, beckoned when he caught her attention. He stepped back when she pushed open the swinging door. "What are you doing?" he asked.

"Getting things ready for C. J. and Cicely's party, of course," she answered easily.

"You said a few things." He pulled her to one side when he saw three waiters headed their way.

She started to tunnel her fingers through her hair, then stopped when she encountered a hairnet. "I'm the maid of honor. It's my responsibility to make sure tonight is everything they want it to be."

He could argue with her not to take on so much, but it wouldn't do any good. "What can I do to help?"

Her relieved smile was almost worth his aggravation at her for taking on so much. "We're pretty busy tonight. You could help me load the trays. The other things are already in the van."

"Other things?"

"I'll explain later." She went though the swinging door.

Summer, with Sin in the passenger seat of the van, parked behind Callahan's Bar a little after six

Saturday night. "I can't wait to see C. J.'s and Cicely's faces. I hope they like what we're doing."

"It has you and a theme. Got to be a hit."

Shaking her head at him, she got out of the van and started for the back. Sin opened the doors, took out a handled bag, and gave it to her. "Those napkins are as heavy as you're going to lift tonight. I called Sam. He and the guys should be waiting to help with the extra chairs and all the things you said the engagement party had to have."

"You'll see that I'm right."

"At least I won't have to lock lips with the hundred or so balloons Dianne found. The helium tank was delivered this morning."

"That might have been interesting to see," she teased.

He grunted. "Go tell Sam to come on out, and I don't want you on a ladder, so don't even think about it if the streamers need adjusting," he told her. "I'll do it. You just point."

Summer made a face. "You're bossy."

"I'm the best man," he said proudly.

"That's debatable," she tossed, then started for the door.

Sin burst out laughing. She gave as good as she got. Somehow his gaze dropped to the enticing sway of rounded hips in the straight ice-blue dress and got stuck there. His body stirred.

He jerked his gaze back up and turned blindly to reach inside the van. Damn. It was happening again!

* * *

An hour later, an excited smile on her face, Summer stood beside Krystal and surveyed their handiwork. They'd all pitched in to transform the restaurant into a romantic, fun setting. At every other table were fat pillar candles tied with the moss-green and petal-pink silk ribbon. On either side of the restaurant's walls were ribbon streamers in the same colors, and at each arch were balloons.

C. J. would get a kick out of the use of the pilsner and shot glasses. Cicely would appreciate the miniature wrought-iron dress frames. By the sign-in book was the memento for Cicely that Sin had suggested, a special arrangement of the white roses sprouting from the dress frame. Summer couldn't believe Sin had come up with the idea. She wouldn't have ever thought that he was sentimental.

"You really know your stuff," Krystal said, her own smile growing.

"Thanks, but we all pitched in to make this happen," Summer said, looking around for Sin. He was with the DJ he'd hired. Strange, he'd been unusually quiet since they began decorating. Where she was, he wasn't. If she didn't know better, she'd think he was avoiding her. Concern for him had her heading in that direction.

"Oh, no."

The horror in those two words from Krystal had Summer swinging back around. Seeing her aunt and uncle coming though the door, she didn't have to ask why the other woman sounded distressed. C. J.'s parents were thirty minutes early. Her stickler-for-etiquette aunt would never dream of showing up that early.

"Excuse me." Summer crossed the room to her aunt and uncle. "Hello, Aunt Evelyn and Uncle Thomas."

"Hello, Summer," they greeted, but her aunt was clearly more interested in the decorations.

Summer hooked her arm through her aunt's. "C. J.'s employees—no, his friends—worked very hard to make this party a success. They did a wonderful job."

Her aunt fingered the satin ribbon dangling from the balloons, studied the white rosebuds draping over the sides of the pilsner glasses, adjusted the position of the shot glasses with the votives around the nine-inch off-white pillar candles, and moved to the rose-covered miniature dress forms before returning to the food. She visibly swallowed on seeing the chocolate mini cupcakes with the initials C&C surrounding the piped-rose cupcakes, forming a heart shape.

Finally, C. J.'s mother turned to Summer and hugged her. "Thank you. Now I'd like to meet C. J.'s friends who decorated the bar so beautifully."

Summer made the introductions, noting that Sin continued talking to the DJ. While C. J.'s parents were talking to Krystal and the other employees,

Summer walked over to Sin. "I hope you told him no Electric Slide."

The lanky man in jeans and a BORN TO LIVE T-shirt grinned. "That's one of my most popular requests."

"C. J.'s parents are here," she said, unable to keep the frown from her face. Sin hadn't looked at her.

After a moment, he responded, "I saw the hug."

For some odd reason, she wanted to give him one. He looked . . . alone. She reached out to touch him, but he turned to the DJ. "C. J. likes Maya and Old School."

The man's uneasy gaze flickered to Summer. "Yeah. I got it covered."

Summer wasn't sure what had just happened, but she did know when she wasn't wanted. She'd deal with the hurt later. "Excuse me."

Chapter 8

Sin watched Summer walk away, her back arrow-straight. He'd seen the hurt confusion in her eyes, heard it in her unsteady voice. He didn't need the censure on the DJ's face to know he'd been rude. His gut was in knots, his emotions as crazy as they'd ever been. He'd slice his arm off before he hurt or embarrass Summer, but that was just what he'd done. He was angry because life had thrown him another unexpected curve.

And he was making her pay for it.

"Play anything fast." He caught up with her a few feet away, took one hand and then the other when he was afraid she'd pull away. Feeling her hands tremble only made him feel worse. "Want to try out the dance floor?"

"Not particularly," she said, her chin up. "Please let me go. I need to check things in the kitchen."

His hands slid up her slim, bare arm; he felt her shiver. *Damn.* "It's me. Never you."

"You two are supposed to be dancing," the DJ called out. "I'll get fired before the gig even begins."

"You don't want to get the man fired, do you?" Sin said, aware he sounded desperate and not caring. The only thing that mattered was removing the shattered look in Summer's eyes. "He has ten children to support."

She stilled, glanced toward the DJ. "You make that up?"

Sin called over his shoulder to the DJ. "Man, how many children do you have?"

"Nine and one on the way. I'm hoping for a boy this time," he called. "Dance or I'm going to play the Electric Slide."

She stared at Sin while his breath caught and his heart beat erratically. He couldn't, wouldn't lose her to these impossible feelings that had blindsided him. "Please."

"You heard the man," she finally said.

Relief swept though him. One hand fell, the other took her hand and spun her away. She watched him as he watched her though the intricate steps. "I never want anything to interfere with our friendship."

"Neither do I."

Yet as he pulled her into his arms, smelled her haunting fragrance, felt the alluring softness of her slim body, he realized things between them had already changed . . . and not for the better.

And he had absolutely no idea how he was going to deal with these unwanted and unexpected feelings.

Seeing Alex and Dianne enter the bar, Sin quickly dropped his arms and stepped back. He was saved. "Alex and Dianne just came in."

Summer looked over her shoulder and hurried to greet them. "Hello, you two. What do you think?"

"Hi. It's even more beautiful than I imagined." Smiling, Dianne glanced around the bar. "You guys did a great job. The color scheme is absolutely perfect."

"Sin, I'd say it was a good thing you knew where to find a helium pump," Alex teased.

"Yeah." Sin slid his hands into the pockets of his slacks. However, it wasn't a good thing that he could still feel the softness of Summer's skin, wanted to feel it again, and so much more. He needed some air.

"Alex, let's go out front and wait for C. J. and Cicely to show up," Sin told him. "For the engagement party, Krystal asked him to park out front instead of in back. She wanted him and Cicely to see the bar for the first time coming though the front door." Without waiting for an answer, Sin walked away.

"What it is?" Alex asked once they were on the sidewalk. "Is it Michael?"

"My brother is fine." Sin worked his shoulders. How had Summer snuck up on him like this?

"Something is bothering you," Alex guessed

"Nothing I can't handle." Sin walked to the edge of the sidewalk and looked down the busy street to a barrage of sounds and lights. He shouldn't still be able to vividly recall the smell of Summer's perfume or recall how it tempted him, making him horny as hell and making him want to go in search of all the sweet, forbidden places on her body where she'd dabbed the fragrance.

His jaw clenched. That kind of thinking wouldn't help. He'd figure out what would, though. There wasn't anything he'd ever put his mind to that he hadn't accomplished. He'd master this as well. "You think C. J. will be fashionably late?"

"Be stubborn, but if you need me, you know I'm there."

Sin angled his head toward Alex. "No offense, but it won't change a thing if things go the way I think they will."

Alex cursed softly. "Stop being so noble. You have friends who would want to be there to help you. You don't have to go through this alone."

Alex was wrong, but Sin knew it would be useless to point it out. He saw the headlights of C. J.'s Bugatti. "They're here." Sin headed back into the bar. "They'll pull up in a minute. Everyone get ready."

The employees of Callahan's Bar stepped forward. Sam, the acting manager while C. J. ran his family's software company, was in front with Krystal. Just behind him were Summer, Sin, Alex, and Dianne. To their left were C. J.'s parents, sister, brother, and his wife. Sin signaled the D.J. and the strong voice of Maya, C. J.'s favorite singer, sounded, singing of a love that went on forever.

Sin had heard the song dozens of time and never thought about the haunting words, but that was before he'd noticed the sweet curve of Summer's mouth, the alluring ones of her body. Unerringly his gaze went to her. Her smile was tentative, unsure. He'd done that. He felt the tightening in his chest.

"Good choice," Summer said.

Sin hesitated, then circled his arm around her waist. She didn't hesitate to do the same. He'd win this battle. He was human. She was a beautiful, desirable woman. She just could never be his woman.

Marriage wasn't in his future, but he wanted this night to be incredible for C. J. and Cicely. Plus, he wanted Summer's memories of him to be happy ones. No matter what, he was determined that they would be.

The front door opened. Cicely came through first with C. J. directly behind her. Her face was flushed. Sin thought C. J. had probably just kissed her. The photographer Sin had hired snapped several shots, then moved aside. Used to the camera, Cicely didn't pay the flash any attention; C. J. paused, then grinned. "I want an eight-by-ten of that one for my desk."

"You got it, man," called the photographer, who promptly took another shot.

Krystal and Sam stepped forward. "Boss . . . C. J. and Cicely, your love is new, but strong. Your friends wish you romance through eternity. Your engagement is the beginning, and we wanted to help you share it with friends and family." Krystal stepped aside as did those behind so C. J. and Cicely could see the decorated bar fully.

"Oh." Cicely palmed her face, but her eyes shone with happiness. "It's beautiful and absolutely perfect."

C. J. hugged her to him. "I hardly recognize the place."

Krystal, who had been smiling, bit her lower lip. C. J. had strong ideas about the atmosphere of his bar. It was a bar, nothing fancy. "Is that good or bad?"

"Good," Cicely answered for him.

C. J. chuckled. "I never thought I'd say it, but definitely good. The place looks great. Thank you." He smiled at his mother. "See, you were worried for nothing."

"And you and Cicely were right," his mother said. "Now let's meet your guests."

Krystal turned to Sin, Summer, Alex, and Dianne as C. J. and Cicely walked away with his parents. "We did it. Thank you."

"You did it," Summer said. "Now let's get this party on the road."

"You're doing it again?" Dianne commented.

"What?" Summer turned with a frown. The party was going well.

Dianne placed her hand on Summer's arm. "Looking at Sin. I admit he's easy on the eyes, but you've never paid him that much attention in the past."

Summer's eyes widened in horror. If Dianne saw her lusting after Sin, perhaps someone else would as well. "I don't know what you mean."

Dianne merely lifted a perfectly arched brow. Summer tucked her head. So, she couldn't bluff. Only Sin didn't mind being her partner when they played cards. Summer's head went even lower. She had to stop thinking about him.

"It's all right. In my opinion, you made a damn good choice."

Summer's head came up. She'd be mortified if Dianne's suspicions went farther. "We aren't dating or anything."

Dianne smiled, her stunning face softened. "Neither were Alex and I or C. J. and Cicely at first, and now look at us. You make a dynamite couple."

Panic coursed through Summer. "You can't tell Alex or anyone."

A frown knitted Dianne's delicate brow. "Take it easy, Summer. You know I'd never break a confidence or spread rumors."

"I know—" Summer bit her lower lip. "It's complicated."

"Not to be redundant, but I think Cicely and I might have thought the same thing."

Summer was already shaking her head before Dianne finished. "This is different. Sin and I are just great friends. He said so himself."

Dianne grunted. "He might not be as smart as I thought."

Summer wasn't sure if she wanted to argue the point or not.

"Well, your great friend is coming this way."

Summer straightened and turned to see Sin a few feet away, a lazy grin on his too-handsome face. "I came to get my dancing partner." Sin caught Summer's hand. "I hate to show C. J. up at his own party, but what the heck."

"I can see it's breaking your heart," Dianne quipped.

Laughing, Sin led Summer onto the dance floor, but as he pulled her into his arms the music changed to a slow song. Sin tensed. He wanted to act as normal as possible, but holding Summer close wasn't a good idea right now.

Sin glanced around and saw C. J. wave. Sin waved back, hoping the grimace on his face passed for a smile.

"You want to sit this one out?" she asked.

He did, but he pulled her into his arms, careful to keep at least a foot of space between them. "The party is a success, thanks to you."

"The credit goes to Krystal and the others."

His head lifted. "I helped load and unload the van, remember."

"I had help preparing the food." He danced well, but that was Sin. He did everything well. If she wasn't careful, she'd get lost in him and the music. Concentrate. "Your party will be just as successful."

"I know." The music ended. Sin stepped back. "I better go see if anyone needs anything."

"Me, too." Summer watched him walk away, aware that he always would.

In the days following, Sin and Summer met almost daily to firm up the plans for his party. She found herself looking forward to those times with him even though there were moments she had to fight her growing attraction to him.

Usually, they'd only see each other occasionally when he was in town—unless he hired her to cater at the stadium or brought clients to Radcliffe's. When he did, he left everything to her.

Sin's unfaltering confidence in her always made her feel extremely proud. He was wealthy enough to hire anyone he wanted. She shouldn't want more from him, had tried to stop herself. It was impossible.

Although she'd promised herself not to be jealous, she'd caught herself a couple of times annoyed at women who were obviously trying to get his attention. Or caught herself staring at his butt in his sinfully tight jeans, which left her feeling hot and rattled. She definitely needed to get out more.

"The party is in two days. Will we be ready?" Sin asked.

"Yes," she answered as they walked toward her restaurant from the florist she'd selected to do the flower arrangements. "I've checked and double-checked. Everything we ordered is in Elegant Decor Events' warehouse and ready to be delivered and set up after four Saturday. Rick and Andy can't wait to show off their culinary skills. The wait staff has been confirmed, with guaranteed backup if needed. The liquor and the margarita machine are scheduled for six."

Sin stopped and drew her out of the flow of traffic. He stared down at her. "This wouldn't have happened without you."

"I know," she said, then grinned. "It was fun."

"It was, wasn't it? Thank you for not laughing when I called a gerbera daisy a carnation."

She twisted her head to one side. "You get points for knowing roses, orchids, and ivy."

He smiled back without thought. She did that, made him smile despite his problems. He could have easily left everything to Summer as he'd always done, but this time he hadn't wanted to. Even though he'd had to fight his unwanted attraction each time they were together, he'd enjoyed being with her.

A couple of times, when he'd stared into her intense chocolate-brown eyes, his thoughts had become tangled. He'd pushed those feelings aside and concentrated on being the friend he'd always been because he sensed something was bothering her as well. She'd never admit it. Together they helped each other forget their worries, if only for a little while.

Summer stirred something in him suspiciously close to need—which, to him, was much more dangerous than desire. However, she was the type of woman who deserved forever. With his family history and his secret, he could never give her that.

Sin shook his head. Summer was way, way off limits. She deserved a man without his baggage. Even as the thought materialized, his hand tightened on her arms. Maybe after the party Saturday night, he'd check in on his other offices and stay away from New York for a while. Not for anything would he hurt her.

She looked up at him in question, patiently waiting for him to say something. He'd shock her if he told her what was on his mind. It scared him how much he wanted to slowly slip off her clothes, taste every incredible inch of her, and then make love to her.

The soft rain hit without warning. Summer shrieked then laughed as Sin grabbed her hand and sprinted the half block to Radcliffe's. Sin expertly dodged people who were trying to get out of the rain just as they were. They were still laughing when they entered the restaurant. The laughter stopped when she slipped in her high heels and he caught her, instinctively drawing her closer, his arms going around her waist to steady her.

For Summer, time stood still as she stared up into Sin's dark eyes swirling with emotions. He'd held her countless times, but she immediately sensed this was infinitely different. This wasn't friend-to-friend, this was man-to-woman. She felt the heat of his body penetrating through her clothes, the muscled hardness of his incredible body. He wanted her. *Sin wanted her.* The knowledge drummed though her body, heating her own blood. Unconsciously, her body softened, and she leaned into him.

Her heart thudded in anticipation as her gaze dropped to the tempting curve of his sensual lips. Air became harder to breathe. If he didn't kiss her, he'd never eat in her restaurant again.

Sin knew desire when he saw it, but he had never expected to see it swirling in Summer's beautiful eyes. The sight stirred a possessiveness in him that he had no business feeling. He'd already had this talk with his brain and another part of his body. She wasn't for him. He was going to set her away from him and get the hell out of there.

It didn't happen.

He didn't know which one moved or if they both did. He only knew he felt the trembling warmth of her soft lips on his. Sweet fire. He was powerless to keep his hands from tightening to bring her closer. He'd wanted before, but he'd never needed like this, as if his very soul depended on the kiss.

Lips-to-lips he tasted her sweetness on his tongue, the passion burning just beneath the surface. It was a lure he couldn't resist.

Summer wrapped her arms around Sin's neck, lifted herself on tiptoes and let his mouth and arms wrap her in pleasure. Her tongue touched his, and fire shot though her, thrilling her. He tasted like her most forbidden dreams, dark and sensual and hot.

Voices of workers in the restaurant intruded. They broke apart at the same time.

Sin blinked, well aware that he wouldn't have stopped on his own. Who would have imagined that Summer, who looked liked an angel, could make his head swim, his body rock-hard. He wanted to feel her soft lips, her tempting body against his again.

If he didn't get out of there, he would.

"I-I'm sorry." Whirling away, he practically ran from the restaurant, from temptation.

A slow smile tilted Summer's lips upward. She stared after Sin. She wasn't the least bit sorry, and in fact was looking forward to more. It appeared the growing attraction she was experiencing wasn't one-sided, as she'd thought. But after Sin's hasty retreat, he didn't appear ready to accept their relationship changing.

The kiss had taken him unawares—which made it that much more special. Sin didn't act on impulse. There was something there, but he was probably rethinking the kiss.

It wouldn't do him any good. She'd always

wanted to be swept away by passion. Sin had done that and more. If he thought he was going to walk away, he'd better think again!

A smile on her face, Summer headed for her office.

Sin was in deep trouble and he knew it.

Ten minutes later, his body was still in overdrive, the intoxicating taste of Summer still on his tongue. The kiss had shattered his control, made desire quicken his blood. This couldn't be happening.

He needed help.

Calling his secretary to tell her he'd be later than expected, he got out of the taxi in front of Alex's office building. If he wasn't in, Sin wasn't sure what he'd do. He just knew he had to put a stop to whatever had just happened. It couldn't happen again. No more kisses. But from the way Summer had been clinging to him, her mouth as greedy as his, she might have a different opinion on the matter.

Sin opened Alex's secretary's door, prepared to charm, to do whatever. He needed to see Alex. "Good morning, Janet."

"Good morning, Mr. Sinclair," she greeted, her fingers poised over a computer keyboard. She brushed the other hand over her stylishly cut salt-and-pepper hair.

"Is Alex available?" Sin's hands fisted in the pockets of his slacks. "It's extremely important."

"I'll call." She reached for the phone and punched in a number. "Mr. Stewart, Mr. Sinclair is here to see you. He says it's important. Yes, sir." She replaced the phone and smiled. "Please go in."

"Thanks." Sin opened Alex's door and almost bumped into him.

"Is everything all right with your brother?" Alex asked.

"It's me," Sin said, then rushed on at the alarm on Alex's face, his hands coming out of his pockets. "No, not that. Something entirely different."

"All right," Alex said, obviously relieved, but clearly puzzled. "It's too early for a drink, and you're too keyed up to sit. I have thirty minutes before my next appointment. You want to take a walk?"

The harmless question brought back Sin's walk with Summer. The shattering kiss they'd shared. "I kissed Summer."

The puzzled expression on Alex's expression didn't change.

Sin shoved his hand over his dark head. "I mean really kissed her, like a man kisses a woman he's interested in."

Alex laughed and slapped Sin on the back. "You sly dog. Summer is a great woman."

"Don't you think I know that?" Sin paced. "That's why I should never have kissed her. You know that better than anyone."

"What I know is that you might be worried for

nothing about the kiss." Alex went to stand beside Sin when he finally stopped and looked out the window.

"Summer is not the type of woman I've dated."

"You mean experienced, empty-headed, star-struck," Alex said. "Women who were impressed with who you were and represented, rather than the man."

Sin frowned at Alex, but he didn't disagree. He had good reasons not to want attachments then or now. "It's best for everyone."

"Sin, stop being so self-sacrificing," Alex snapped. "You can't go on denying yourself happiness because of what *might* happen. I don't think Summer has dated very much, but she has her head on straight. A kiss doesn't mean you're headed for the altar."

Sin's eyes narrowed and Alex muttered under his breath. Sin had said almost the same thing to C. J. to goad him into realizing he loved Cicely.

"Not my best argument." Alex shook his head.

"Because you care about all parties involved, and you're a good friend." Sin slid his hands back into the pockets of his slacks. "I don't want Summer hurt."

"Maybe you're reading too much into the kiss. Maybe she's forgotten all about it," Alex said.

Sin didn't see how that was possible. He certainly hadn't. He vividly remembered the rose-petal softness of her lips, the initial shyness of her tongue against his, then the erotic boldness. Her exquisite breasts pressed against his chest, the slender length of her body fitting so perfectly to his, the—

Alex cleared his throat. "I guess not, huh?

Sin hoped he wasn't blushing, and glanced away. "She'll remember."

"And so will you." It was a statement, not a question.

"Yes," Sin admitted.

"Then give both of you a chance to see what develops afterward," Alex told him. "For once, date someone you're not going through the motions with."

Sin shook his dark head. "If it was anyone but Summer, I might."

"I think you're making a mistake."

"Won't be my first or last." Sin headed for the door. He was definitely leaving New York on Sunday on his private jet after the Yankee game. He wasn't taken any chance of letting things get out of hand with Summer. In the meantime, maybe it was best that he saw her as little as possible. There was no sense tempting fate. "See you and Dianne Saturday night."

"We'll be there," Alex said. "And Sin?"

His hand on the knob, Sin turned. "Yes?"

"Nobility is overrated, but never a true friend and never a woman who cares about you."

Sin nodded to acknowledge he'd heard what Alex said, then continued out the outer office and down the hall toward the elevators. Alex meant well, but he hadn't lived with the burden all these years. Sin was different and, no matter how he wished and prayed, his mind and body might turn on him one day. And there wasn't a thing anyone could do to prevent it from happening.

Friday afternoon, Summer stared at the phone on her desk, drummed her nails on the polished surface. She hadn't heard from Sin since the kiss. She wrinkled her nose. Just as she'd thought. He was avoiding her.

Picking up the phone, she called Sin's office. It was time to take matters into her own hands.

"Sinclair Management, Mrs. Douglas speaking," answered a crisp female voice.

"Hello, Mrs. Douglas. This is Summer Radcliffe. May I speak to Mr. Sinclair?"

"I'm sorry, Ms. Radcliffe, he's in a conference and asked not to be disturbed. Is there a message?"

Of course there had been times that he really hadn't been able to speak with her, but Summer was suspicious that this wasn't one of them. "I just wanted to go over the final details of the party with him. Please have him call me at his earliest convenience."

"I will, Ms. Radcliffe," Mrs. Douglas said. "I'm looking forward to coming. Mr. Sinclair said you were fantastic at planning events. He has high praise for you."

Summer wished that was enough. "Thank you.

Good-bye." She hung up the phone. "Sin, you can run, but you can't hide."

Friday night Sin stood at the window of his penthouse staring out the window, his hands deep in the pockets of his dress slacks. Life had kicked him in the teeth again, taken what never could be replaced.

Summer.

His eyes briefly shut, then opened. He turned away from the window and headed for the bar across the room. Perhaps a scotch would help erase the picture of Summer, soft and clinging in his arms; erase the sweetness of her mouth that quickly blazed into passion.

He picked up the squat bottle, uncapped the crystal top, then set the bottle down and recapped it. Drinking would solve nothing. He'd seen too many men start down that road. He just wished he knew what would help.

Summer.

He went to the bedroom to grab his jacket and house keys. It was a little after 9:00 PM; maybe C. J. was at Callahan's. Cicely was on assignment in Miami. Beating C. J. at pool would lighten his mood.

Downstairs, he grabbed a cab and gave the bar's address, aware that that wasn't where he wanted to go. Playing pool wasn't what he wanted to be doing.

He stared aimlessly out the window at the street light, the people. No matter the catastrophe, life went on around you. The thought somehow made him feel sadder.

The cab came to a screeching stop in front of Callahan's. Seeing the lighted sign did nothing to elevate Sin's crappy mood. Paying the driver, he got out and went inside. He was greeted by Maya's strong, breathy voice over the loudspeaker. He listened to the unhappy lyrics about the pitfalls of falling in love, the unexpected pleasure and pain. They sent a sharp jab to his midsection.

Seeing C. J. at the bar, Sin moved in that direction. Nodding to Krystal as she went by with a tray of food and drinks, he slid onto a stool. "What do your regulars say about the balloons and ribbon nailed on the beam over the cash register?" Sin asked when C. J. moved to him.

"That I'm a lucky SOB since they've seen Cicely." C. J. reached for a longneck and placed it in front of Sin. "If I didn't know better, I'd think you had a woman problem."

Sin couldn't help the start of guilty surprise.

C. J. slapped Sin on the back. "I'll be damned. I better not be the last one to know." Rounding the bar, he took Sin by the arm. "Details."

Sin grabbed the beer to break eye contact. Hell, he hated being dishonest with his oldest friend. The truth would end that friendship or at least put a strain on it. "There aren't any. I guess the party tomorrow night has me a little tense."

Hands on his hips, C. J. stared down at Sin as he

slid into the booth. "Don't think that's it. I've seen that look before. Spill."

Sin tilted the bottle of beer to his mouth. C. J. was always too perceptive.

Finally, C. J. slid into the other side of the booth. "Falling in love blindsided me, so I'll let you off the hook. But since you're part of the reason I finally stopped fighting the fact that I love Cicely, I'm here for you when you're ready."

Sin glanced behind them. No one was at the pool table. "How about a game?"

"You sure you can handle being beaten at pool plus what's really bothering you?" C. J. asked.

Sin almost smiled. He was glad he'd come. "You sure you can handle being beaten while missing Cicely?"

C. J. leaned over the table, his eyes intent. "If anyone had told me two months ago I'd now be crazy in love, I would have laughed my head off, then found a woman to prove him wrong. But here I am, and I wouldn't change a thing. I count the hours Cicely is away and thank God for every one she's with me."

"Forever isn't for everyone," Sin said softly, his hand clutching the bottle.

"You're not everyone. You're Payton Scott Sinclair, a man to be reckoned with, and you're almost as good looking as I am," C. J. finished.

Sin burst out laughing. "I told Summer about your big head." The words came out easily, but the sudden need to see her wasn't so easy to deal with.

"I call it the way I see it."

"Hey, Sin," Krystal greeted. "Boss, Cicely is on the phone."

A grin flashed across C. J.'s face. He began to scoot out of the booth. "This might take a while."

"Go." Sin tilted his beer. "Tell her I said hello."

Standing, C. J. clapped Sin on the back. "Women have always come easy to us, maybe too easy. I didn't like it very much when Summer said it to me, but I accepted the truth. That's why when a woman changes the rules, it's so hard to accept. Just because it's different doesn't mean it's not right. 'Night."

"'Night." Sin watched C. J. walk at a fast clip toward his office, heard the good-natured teasing from a few men at the bar who apparently knew the reason. C. J. just waved and walked faster. Standing, Sin put a twenty on the table and headed for the door.

Different didn't begin to explain the problem. He hadn't believed a kiss could be dangerous. He now knew differently.

Summer wasn't just any woman. She was forbidden to him any way he looked at the situation, but that didn't seem to matter to his stubborn heart. He was falling in love with her, and it was killing him.

Chapter 9

Summer arrived a little after three Saturday afternoon to begin preparations for the party. Her stomach was doing a three-step. She couldn't believe she was this nervous. Sin had never returned her call—which confirmed her suspicion that he regretted the kiss.

If she didn't strongly feel that he was trying to be noble, she would really be annoyed with him. After waiting thirty years for a man to make her weak in the knees, forget to breathe with a kiss, she was anxious for more of the same.

Her hand gripped the overnight case in one hand, the padded hangers with her clothes for the party in the other. Party first, and then she was going to get herself another kiss—and if she was lucky, maybe a lot more.

Blushing and grinning, she pushed the doorbell and prepared herself for the punch of seeing Sin again . . . if he didn't chicken out and stay in his home office.

The door opened. Sin stood there, his handsome

fallen-angel face set. Her heart thudded. *Looks like no kiss.*

"Hi, Sin." Summer greeted him with a cheery smile despite the growing nervousness in her stomach. She stepped past him into his penthouse. "The florists should be here within the hour. Elegant Decor Events will follow with linens, chairs, tables, plates, and service ware. My people will be here shortly thereafter to start getting the food together."

His gaze flickered to the overnight case, the garment bag. "It occurred to me that it's asking a great deal of you to be my hostess. I've taken you away from Radcliffe's enough. I could probably manage."

Her fingers flexed on the handle of the leather case. "Then you suddenly know how to arrange flowers and where to place them, which serving pieces to use, how to organize the buffet tables, and how to prepare food besides coffee?"

"No, but I could probably get someone," he said without skipping a beat.

She'd punch him if he didn't look so miserable. "Who? Where?"

"I could probably make a few phone calls."

Stubborn man, but then so was she. "Haven't you learned yet?"

A frown worked its way across his brow. "Learned what?"

"I'm a one of a kind." She turned and headed for the stairs. "I'll put my things in the guest bedroom and be right back." At the top of the stairs she stopped and stared back. He hadn't moved. Her heart went out to him. "It will be all right, Sin."

"I'll be in my office." He turned and headed across the expanse of imported Italian tile.

Summer stared after him for a moment, then continued up the stairs. She had a party to put together.

With so many people there to assist Summer, Sin stayed in his office. He only emerged to answer the door as different services came and went. Summer had been right: He would have been lost in directing everyone. She did it effortlessly and always with a smile.

As the evening lengthened, he had to admire the way the place came together with the addition of the tables for four on the terrace set with bold floral arrangement of red poppies, more flower arrangements around the great room, candles, splashes of red and orange. There were more subtle differences, all of them due to Summer.

He wandered over to the orchids spilling from a row of slim cylindrical crystal vases on the entrance table, the candles in front—elegant and beautiful, just like Summer. Sin blew out a disgusted breath. How did she slip past his defenses? One kiss shouldn't have impacted him this way. Hell, he'd discovered girls in the fifth grade. Women did not knock him off his stride, did not make him restless.

Unless that woman was Summer Radcliffe.

He headed for his office. He'd considered leaving, but that would have been even more cowardly than hiding. Summer was taking time from her busy schedule to help him. She just didn't know she was making him crazy. He heard her voice, soft and happy, and quickened his steps. He shut the door, wishing he could just as easily shut off his growing need for her.

Later that afternoon Summer stood outside of Sin's office door. He'd hidden from her since she'd arrived. Sin wasn't the type of man to let others come into his home and not personally see what they were doing. When he'd moved into the penthouse, he'd supervised every piece being loaded, unloaded, and then its placement. He'd worked just as hard as the movers. Before the kiss, she'd fully expected him to be there looking over her and the workers' shoulders just as he had when they were making the final plans for his party

Her annoyance had morphed into concern as the day lengthened. Sin also wasn't the type of man not to face his problems. The next logical conclusion was that this situation between them was as new for him as it was for her.

She'd given him time to get over the apparent shock of their attraction, but now it was time to see where they went from here. She knocked on the door.

*   *   *

Sin didn't jump when he heard the knock, but his heart did. He knew that soft knock. He glanced at the crystal clock on his desk: 7:03 PM. Guests were due to arrive at eight, but they could come early.

He glanced down at the new contract of one of his clients, Cameron McBride. Sin couldn't recall two details of the twenty-odd pages. He'd accomplished absolutely nothing since he'd been in his office. "Come in."

The door opened. Summer took two steps in and stopped, her hand still on the knob. "Would you like to see if you approve of how things turned out? If you'd like to change anything?"

"I trust you."

"Sin, get off your butt and come out of this office." Releasing the door, she took another two steps. "This is *your* event. The least you could do is take the time to see how things look."

Sin might have smiled at any other time. Summer didn't pull punches. She was a woman to reckon with. She just could never be *his* woman.

He got to his feet. If possible, he wasn't going to lose her friendship. "I saw the flower arrangements and the extra seating on the terrace, the lighting. It all looks great."

"You haven't see the buffet settings, tested the margarita from the machine, seen the unique toppings for the desserts, spoken to the extra staff hired to make this night appear seamless." Going to him, she circled her arm through his. His arm brushed against her breast. He jumped, his gaze snapped to hers.

She swallowed, stared straight ahead. "Come on. I have to shower and get dressed to be ready in time to meet your guests, and you have to get dressed as well."

Sin followed Summer out of his office thinking he could have done without the reminder that she would be showering, water caressing her luscious, naked body, something he was destined never to do.

Summer dressed in a cutout white blouse, blue jeans, belt, and blue cowboy boots. Taking her hair down, she combed it around her shoulders. When she turned her head, her gold hoop earrings brushed against her cheeks.

She'd never thought of tempting a man, but she planned on tempting Sin. For a moment she wished the party had been formal. She had a Valentino gown that was pure sin. A secret smile on her lips, she left her room just as Sin was coming out of his.

He'd opted for a white shirt and blue jeans as well. His shirt cuffs were rolled up. Summer saw the flash of desire in Sin's eyes before he could mask the emotion, and breathed easier for the first time since she arrived.

The doorbell rang. She extended her arm. "George is answering the door, and the waiters are there with margaritas, mojitos, and beer, or to take orders, but we should be there to greet your guests."

After a moment's hesitation, he stepped forward to take her arm, careful to keep their bodies separated, and started for the stairs.

Summer inwardly sighed. She wasn't giving up. Sin had taught her to go after what she wanted.

Now that she knew he cared, she was going after him. Before the night was up she was getting that kiss.

Sin mingled with his guests, pleased that the party was going well even if he couldn't shake the tension, the fact that he felt a bit off. With a bar inside and one on the terrace, and staff circulating to assist with filling food and drink requests, wait time for either was a minimum.

Of course there were the usual clusters of people who knew one another or who were in the same sport, but for the most part guests were mingling and scattered from the great room to the terrace. Several couples were dancing on the terrace beneath the canopy of twinkling lights, while others were at one of the round tables eating or chatting. At any other time he and Summer would have been the first to hit the dance floor.

He couldn't chance it. He wanted her too badly, was too close to the edge.

His hand flexed on the bottle of beer in his hand. He hadn't taken one sip. It wasn't what he wanted, what he could never have.

"Nice party, Payton. Thank for the invite."

Sin put on his game face and smiled at Lucas
Jones, the starting quarterback for one of the best
teams in the NFL. He'd joined the team as a free
agent from Tennessee and stepped into the lineup
after the veteran quarterback dislocated his shoulder midway through last season.

Sin glanced at the tall glass of nonalcoholic san-
gria in Lucas's long-fingered hand. "I'm glad you
could come."

"Me, too."

Sin caught the change in Lucas's voice, the rapt
expression in his boyish face. He was staring at
Summer with the unmistakable fascination of a man
interested in a woman as she moved from guest to
guest, making sure they were having a good time.
Not once had Sin seen her still for more than a few
minutes since the first guest arrived.

"That is one beautiful woman." Lucas turned
to him. "Sims says you've known each other a long
time."

Sims was Lucas's agent. "Yes," Sin answered,
already knowing what was coming next.

"Do you think she's seeing someone?" Lucas's
attention shifted to Summer once again as if he
couldn't keep his eyes off her. "I'd like to ask her
out."

No screamed in Sin's head. He wasn't surprised
to find his hand clenched on the bottle of beer in his
hand. It didn't matter that Lucas was a nice guy,
and surprisingly levelheaded and honest.

"I guess you not answering says it all." Lucas took a sip of his drink. "It was a long shot someone that beautiful wasn't attached."

All he had to do was keep quiet. "She's not seeing anyone."

Lucas whipped around with the quickness that enabled him to evade and scramble for yardage, to connect with his receiver downfield. "You're sure?"

Sin tried to smile and found his muscles wouldn't cooperate. He wanted her to be happy, so why did he feel like his heart was being ripped from his chest? "I'm sure."

"Excuse me."

Sin watched the man head straight for Summer. As much as he wanted to look away, he couldn't.

"Excuse me, please."

Summer turned with a smile to see the young man she recognized as a rising star in the NFL. He quickly removed his black Stetson. "Hi, Lucas. Is there something I can do for you?"

"As a matter of fact there is."

"Yes?" she urged when he didn't continue.

He held the hat to his chest. "Would you like to go out with me?"

Summer was completely thrown by the request.

Lucas shifted nervously. "I guess Payton was wrong about you not seeing someone."

She finally found her tongue. "You asked him about me?"

"I didn't want to step on anyone's toes," he quickly explained. "He said you weren't seeing anyone. I should have known he was wrong. You're too beautiful not to be taken."

Summer looked beyond Lucas to Sin standing by himself. His jaw was clenched. His eyes were narrowed dangerously. He wasn't happy about Lucas, but he'd sent him just the same. He was being noble again. "Sin was right, but I'm too busy running my restaurant to think about dating. I'm flattered that you asked me, though."

"My agent told me about your restaurant," Lucas said. "He said it's one of the best in the city. The next time I'm here, I'd like to stop by if I can get reservations."

She liked the handsome young man. He wasn't obnoxious and he didn't have an ego the size of the Empire State Building. Just the kind of man Krystal needed. "Please ask for me when you call, and I'll make it happen."

He shook his head, starring down at her in puzzlement. "The men in New York must be pitiful to let you roam free."

She leaned closer. "They don't let me. It's my choice."

He burst out laughing. She joined him.

Sin, you might be in more trouble than you thought, Alex mused as he sipped his black mojito. In the past, Sin had never been possessive about a woman or watched her like he couldn't get enough of her. For a moment, Alex thought he might have to stop Sin from hurting one of his clients. He watched Lucas talking to Summer as if he wanted to break every bone in the young man's body.

His easygoing, no-attachment friend had it bad and was doing his best to fight his feelings. Alex hoped he failed. If Sin was right about his brother's illness, he needed Summer more than ever.

Standing with Alex were Dianne, C. J., and Cicely. The women had strawberry margaritas and were chatting about Cicely's recent trip to Miami for the Mercedes Swim Fashion Week. Alex hoped he handled Dianne's travels as well as C. J. when Dianne had to travel with their fashion line in the coming months.

Everyone in his family and extended family made it a point never to sleep apart. That he might be the first wasn't a comforting thought. But neither was stopping Dianne from living her dream. He'd do whatever it took to make their marriage work, and staring down at her as she looked up at him, he knew she'd do the same. Love sometimes required sacrifices, but the rewards were well worth it.

Switching his attention back to Sin, Alex was reminded of himself watching Dianne and feeling hopeless that she'd ever feel anything more than friendship for him; of C. J. watching Cicely and fighting his feelings tooth and nail. It appeared Sin was doing the same.

It wouldn't do Sin any good, Alex thought. Some things were just meant to be, and as he'd told Sin once, you can't tell your heart who to love.

Alex, however, was not about to point out the obvious to his friend. Sin was dealing with enough because of his brother. Sin just hadn't realized he didn't have to face it alone.

Alex would keep his opinion to himself. Summer had guts. She had to, to open Radcliffe's and make it a success. Life had kicked both of them in the teeth at an early age with the loss of their parents. Both had succeeded despite their family tragedies. Both deserved someone to love them unconditionally.

Alex glanced over at C. J. and recognized the hard frown on his face, the narrowed gaze. He was in full protective mode. Even with all the activity of the party—including two buffet and dessert stations, two bar areas, tables and dancing on the terrace— he, too, had noticed Sin looking at Summer, his eyes hot and needy.

"Excuse me," C. J. said as he started toward Sin.

"Excuse me," Alex said, catching C. J. and leading him in the opposite direction of Sin. "Have you seen the way she's looking at him?"

C. J. jerked his head toward Summer, who was just leaving a group of woman, her gaze on Sin just as needy and hot. C. J. cursed under his breath.

"Exactly," said Alex. "We've seen the same expression when we look in the mirror. Neither one of them needs your interference."

"That's why he came to the bar last night so torn up. I never saw this coming," C. J. said.

"I don't think they did, either," Alex mused. "Sin would walk through hell to keep from hurting Summer. We both trust him with our lives."

C. J.'s eyes narrowed. "If Sin causes her one moment of unhappiness, I'm going to beat the hell out of him."

From across the room, Sin had seen C. J. start for him and Alex stop him. C. J. now knew the woman who was causing Sin's problems was Summer. Since C. J. wasn't in Sin's face and one of them wasn't on the floor bleeding, whatever Alex had said must have partially alleviated C. J.'s concern. However, he still looked as if he'd gladly break every bone in his best friend's body if he harmed Summer.

Sin expected no less. He would have done the same thing to any man who took advantage of her. That's why he was keeping his hands to himself no matter how much he wished things were different or how many signals she sent him.

Sin watched Cicely and Dianne join the men, then continue toward him. "Having a good time?" he asked.

"Fantastic," Cicely said. "Since C. J. got to wear jeans, he's a happy camper as well."

Sin's lazy gaze moved to C. J. His body might not be safe after all. "Is that right?"

Before he could answer, Summer joined them, looping her arm through Sin's and leaning against him. He felt the softness of her breast and barely kept from groaning.

His hand tightened on the longneck.

"Yep, I'm having a great time."

Sin's gaze swung to C. J.'s. His best friend had a grin on his face. He was giving Sin a pass. Sin's desperate gaze moved to Alex, begging for help. He kissed his wife's hand. Sin wanted to cry that forever wasn't for him.

"Summer, Sin. This is the best party I've been to in years." Dianne lifted her margarita. "The food is delicious. That was my first time eating flan. I blew my diet."

'We can dance it off," Alex suggested.

Cicely laughed. "C. J. and I would be dancing all night. I couldn't resist the apple pie with the brandy butter sauce and ice cream."

"Well, I'm going back for more tortilla chips and queso. I'm considering adding them to the appetizer menu at the bar. That's good stuff," C. J. said.

"Thank you," Summer said, pleased. "Excuse us, we have to circulate, then I have to check on the kitchen."

"You should be enjoying yourself." Sin frowned. "You've been on your feet since you arrived this afternoon. You haven't even danced."

She smiled at him. "Did you forget this is what I do? I enjoy seeing people having a good time and eating good food. We'll dance later. Now, excuse us."

Sin allowed her to lead him away. He was in trouble and sinking deeper.

The party was all he had hoped for and more. Sin could see it in the smiling faces as his guests reluctantly started to leave around twelve. A waiter held a basket of wrapped pralines toward them as they exited.

Sin shook hands with the last couple, Ross and Debra Yarbrough, a little after one. Ross was a point guard in the NBA. "Thank you for coming."

"Thank you," Debra said, holding up a praline. "I had a great time without all the drama that sometimes goes on with the parties we attend."

"Yeah," Ross said. "It was nice just to relax and have fun."

"That's what Sin wanted," Summer said from beside him. "I'm glad you enjoyed yourselves."

"We did. Good night."

"Good night." Sin closed the door, prepared to get rid of Summer, but she was already walking away.

"The caterers can clean up. You've done enough. I'll write your check," he called.

"No hurry on the check." She kept walking. "Everyone needs to clean up and take their things with them. You can go to bed. I can let myself out."

She knew he wasn't about to go to bed and leave

her up working. She was just being stubborn. Well, she'd soon learn that he wouldn't be ignored. In his study, he sat behind his desk and wrote out her check, adding a sizable bonus. There would be no more need for her to contact him.

Ignoring the tightness in his chest, he quickly tore out the check and stood. He'd give it to her in front of the people who were cleaning up, dismissing her. There would be no reason for her to stay. He'd . . .

He plopped down in his chair. He wouldn't, couldn't be that cruel to her. She was tempting him more than he thought possible, but she was also trying to do the impossible, help him.

His fate had been sealed the day he was born and there was nothing she or anyone else could do about it.

Summer thanked the last of the catering team and closed the door of Sin's penthouse. The hardest task was ahead, facing Sin and getting that kiss. Or two. He hadn't even danced with her.

Her legs were a bit unsteady, but she continued to his office. If it was any other man, she wouldn't be pushing this. With Sin, it was different. She knew him, trusted him, and now she was falling in love with him.

She'd waited so long to feel the almost giddy emotions of falling in love, she wasn't about to turn her back on them. Yet, even more, she sensed that he needed her. He might not want to admit it, but when those painful shadows darkened his eyes, he had reached for her.

She knocked on his office door. Silence. She didn't waste time knocking again. She opened the door.

From across the room their gaze met, clung. She felt his pain and started for him. "Sin."

"I don't want to want you," he said. "Go home." Cruel words to be sure, but they were better than the alternative.

Summer never paused. Rounding the desk, she sat in his lap and tucked his head against her breasts, holding him to her, asking for nothing, giving him everything he wanted and could never have.

"I'm where I want to be." Her hand stroked his back. "I'm here. It's all right."

"It's not." Removing her arms from around his neck, he set her on her feet and handed her the check. "Thank you, Summer. You did a wonderful job."

She stared at him, completely ignoring the check. "Why are you fighting this so hard?"

He should have known she would be direct and not be easily swayed. Summer went after what she wanted, always had, always would. "You deserve what I can't give you."

Her eyebrow lifted, then she pointedly glanced down. There was no way she could miss the bulge in his jeans. Especially when he hardened even more. He wanted her with a desperation that was killing him.

Taking her arm, he placed the check in her hand. He was hanging by a thread. *Please leave.* "Thank you."

Her hand fisted over the check. Her eyes narrowed in anger. Lips he hungered to taste again, tightened. "Too bad I can't say the same." Turning, she stalked from the room without a backward glance, closing the door softly after her. Summer didn't blow when she was angry; she seethed. She was furious with him, but he had accomplished want he wanted, needed to do. He'd put an end to whatever craziness it was between them.

So why did he feel as if someone had ripped him open?

Because he had done the very thing he wanted to avoid: He'd hurt her. Sitting behind his desk, he propped his elbows on the cluttered surface and let his forehead rest in his open palms. He negotiated multimillion-dollar contracts, got perks that were unheard of. He knew the power of persuasion, how to charm and cajole.

None of that mattered, because this time his emotions were involved. He enjoyed what he did, but he knew he wouldn't always come out the winner. When those infrequent times happened, he'd always walked away with a clear conscience that he'd done his best.

That wasn't possible this time. He'd handled

things wrong. Worse, he'd been more worried about himself than he had about Summer. That angered him the most. He was protecting himself. Every time he'd looked into her eyes tonight, felt her body against his, he'd felt himself getting in deeper. To protect himself, he'd given her a check when she had given him peace of mind.

He hadn't even told her that he'd arranged a car to take her home. He needed his butt kicked.

Sin came out of his chair like a shot. Opening the door, he went up the stairs and caught her coming out of the guest bedroom. "Summer." She walked past him. He wasn't surprised. She had a right to be pissed with him.

He sprinted to her. "A car is waiting to take you home."

"I can get a cab." His hand closed over hers, stopping her. He felt hers tremble, then firm.

"There are some things going on in my life now," he admitted. "There's no room for anything else."

She turned and looked up at him, patience and caring shining back at him. "We could go sit on the terrace or walk out there. It's spacious enough."

She might turn him inside out, but he wouldn't have missed having her in his life. She was a woman a man could count on. She just could never be more to him. She needed to understand that and move on without him.

Taking her overnight case and garment bag, he

placed them on a chair by the wide stairwell, then pulled her to a small sofa overlooking the first floor and sat down. "I didn't intend for this to happen."

"It was a shock to me as well." Her smile was sweet, hopeful.

Sin took a deep breath and plunged ahead. He needed to get this over with quickly. She tempted him more than he thought a woman could. "I will never marry, never have a family." His hands flexed on his thighs. "It wouldn't be fair to you have an affair with me."

"I don't remember asking you to marry me."

Stunned by her response, he jerked his head around and stared at her.

"Sin, I realize this isn't the norm for you. It's a first for me, but it's as I told Lucas, I'm too busy running Radcliffe's to date."

His eyes blazed. "You were laughing with him."

Her hand covered his clenched fist. "And thinking he might be the right man for Krystal. I've already picked out the man for me."

"Didn't you hear what I said?" he asked tightly. "I won't be around for the long haul. It would be just sex between us."

Her hand lifted to palm his cheek. "If the kiss is any indication, I'd say you're wrong."

He caught her hand, intending to move it away, but clutched it instead. Just like her to try to reassure him and turn him inside out in the process. "I can't be what you need, what you deserve."

She leaned closer, her warm, intoxicating breath fanning his face. "You're exactly what I want. Perhaps this will help you believe."

Her lips softly touched his; her tongue outlined the seam of his mouth. He shuddered. His hands lifted to grab her arms. He didn't know whether he wanted to draw her closer or push her away.

Her tongue slipped inside his mouth to tenderly stroke his—giving without asking in return. That kind of selflessness rocked him, left him defenseless. Need burst through him.

His hands pulled her closer. She went willingly, the softness and warmth of her body wrapped around him, comforting him, exciting him. He was lost, and yet, somehow, the taste and feel of her seemed more right that anything in his life.

With that certainty locked in his mind, his mouth locked on hers, he picked her up in his arms. By pure instinct, by driving need he found his bedroom and the bed he'd never thought of bringing another woman to. Only Summer. Slowly he set her to her feet and lifted his head. His breath gushed over his lips. Hers wasn't any steadier.

His hands trembled as he palmed her face, stared into her eyes a bit dazed with passion. He wanted to speak, to tell her how beautiful she was, how much he wanted her.

"Sin."

His name trembled over her lips with such need and trust that words no longer seemed necessary.

His hands in her glorious hair, he kissed her again, letting the hunger he'd tried so long to control run free.

She kissed him back the same wild way, her tongue dancing with his, heating his body, hardening him. His mouth moved from her lips to the sweet curve of her jaw, then downward to encounter her blouse.

He wanted to rip the offending material away. His eyes shut as he drew in a steadying, calming breath. He'd make this special for Summer if it killed him.

He reached for the buttons of her blouse, felt her hands doing the same with his shirt. Parting the white material, his breath snagged on seeing her high, firm breasts in the lacy white bra. His thumb traced over the dark, distended nipple, felt it harden, felt her tremble.

He had to taste her. He couldn't wait. His head lowered, taking the tight bud into his mouth. His tongue laved the point, suckled. Her back arched, her hand curved around his head, holding him closer. She tasted better than his fantasy.

"Sin." His name came out on a needy moan, a hiss of pleasure. She trembled in his arms.

Torn between continuing and getting them undressed, he fought to lift his head and allowed her to sit on the side of the bed, then dropped to his knees and quickly removed her boots. If he didn't make love to her soon, he'd either explode or go crazy.

Unbuckling her belt, he pulled off her jeans. Finished, on his knees in front of her, he just stared at her beautiful flushed face, her glorious black hair tumbled around her shoulders, the tiny patch of white cloth covering her breasts, covering the most intimate part of her, covering where he wanted to be. He wanted their first time to be incredible, special.

If he was to pay emotionally for his lapse, he'd make it good for both of them

Pushing to his feet, he ripped off the shirt she'd unbuttoned, then got rid of his shoes, briefs, and jeans. On his knees again, he kissed the inside of her thigh and worked his way up her quivering stomach to her breasts. Unhooking the front fastener of her bra, he pulled the white lace away, his eyes glued to the rise of fall of the lush mounds.

His head lowered, his mouth opened.

She closed her eyes as his warm mouth closed over her nipple, his finger and thumb teasing the other nipple as twin assaults of pleasure rocked her. She'd never imagined anything this good, this intense.

His hand moved from her breast and she wanted to cry out at the loss until he cupped her where she ached for him. Instinctively she moved against his hand. When he tugged at the elastic band of her panties, she eagerly lifted her hips. The material had no more left her legs than his hand was there again, this time stroking her intimately.

She moaned his name, clutched at his arms as his mouth and hand made her burn with need, with pleasure. Emotions swamped her.

His incredible mouth was on hers again, his tongue deep and erotic, driving her higher, higher still, while his hand stroked her relentlessly, making her hips move shamelessly, and all she could think of was she wanted more.

And he gave it to her.

His head lifted. She stared into his eyes, blazing with passion, as his hands slid under her hips. Her body hummed, fire licking low in her belly. His mouth covered hers as did his body when he began to enter her.

He closed his eyes as exquisite sensation rocked him. He tried to draw in a controlling breath at the tight fit, felt the resistance. His eyes snapped open as realization dawned.

She was a virgin. He had to stop.

Her eyes opened. Sensuality and hunger stared back at him. Her arm hooked around his neck the same time she lifted her hips, wrapped her legs around him, and fastened her mouth to his. He was lost. His hips surged forward, bringing them together, again and again. He caught her small gasp in his mouth. She clenched around him.

Power and sensations ripped though him as he loved her, stroked her. Her eyes half closed, her lips slightly party, her hair tumbled over his pillow as she welcomed him into her body again and again.

He'd remember the glorious sight always. He'd remember and cherish the night she was his.

Then he felt her clench, spasm around him. Thinking became impossible as he answered the call of her body. She went over, taking him with her in her wild, sweet fire.

Chapter 10

Later when he could draw in a full breath, when his senses cleared, Sin lay with Summer wrapped in his arms, wishing he could keep her there. But no woman would want a man who couldn't have children, who possibly carried a horrible hereditary disease.

She was his one weakness. A small voice told him somehow he'd always known she would be. Yet he had to be strong for her.

How he was going to end this? The question pounded in his brain. He had no idea, especially when he wanted nothing more than to keep holding her, to love her again and shut out the world. That wasn't about to happen. For her sake, this ended now.

He eased her away from him, but she climbed, naked, warm, and tempting, on top of him, placed her head on his chest, began making lazy strokes with her fingertips on his chest, her hair grazing over him. He clenched his fists to keep from stroking the long, curly strands.

"If I had known it would be this incredible, I

wouldn't have waited twelve years." She lifted her head slightly, a winsome smile curving her lips swollen from his kisses. "I had a crush on you when I was eighteen."

"Summer—"

"It's all right. You didn't know, and I would have been mortified if you had." She briefly placed her fingertips to his lips and lay down on his chest again. "I guess every woman fantasizes, dreams about her first time."

He was compelled to ask. "Did you?"

He felt her nod. "I wanted to be swept away by the mindless passion that I'd heard and read so much about. But I wanted it with a man I respected and cared for, a man who might get a little swept away himself."

"I should have stopped." There was regret and recrimination in his tortured voice.

"But don't you see? That's what made it so wonderful. I knew from that first kiss in the entrance of Radcliffe's that that man would be you."

He stiffened. A dangerous kiss had begun his downfall.

The hand making lazy strokes paused, her head slowly lifted, and she stared down at him. Sin knew there was no way to mask his anger at his own weakness then and now, making love with her when he knew she had no future with him.

He should have his butt kicked. No doubt, C. J. would do the job.

Her eyes widened in horror and embarrassment. She rolled off him. On her knees, she wrapped the sheet around her breasts and bit her lower lip. "I'm sorry, Sin. It was probably horrible for you." She swallowed and started scooting off the bed.

The thought that her leaving would solve his problem lasted only a split second. The price was too high. He caught her arm, saw the sheen of tears in her eyes just before she lowered her head. The sight sliced though him. "You move me. You always have." His hand flexed on her bare arm. "The gift of your innocence . . . words can't describe how much it meant to me. I've never felt this way about a woman, but it shouldn't have happened. Don't let me hurt you. Please."

Her head lifted and so did her arm, letting the sheet fall, baring her breasts. She didn't seem to notice. She cupped his face, stared into the turbulence in his eyes. "Sin, please don't worry. I know this isn't forever. I have my life and you have yours. For a little while we'll enjoy the pleasure of each other's company, and when it's over, we'll still be friends."

"You're too innocent and too inexperienced to realize that intimacy changes things." His expression hardened. "I'd rather have you as a friend than as a lover."

"Really?"

"Really." As long as the sheet covered his erection and she stayed where she was, he might pull this off.

She smiled, sexy, knowing. Sin knew he was in trouble, but before he could move, she had one arm around his neck, nibbling, kissing, as her hand closed around him. "Say that again," she practically purred.

He might if he could have formed a coherent thought; then she straddled him. Weak fool that he was, he joined the two of them once again, sighed with the intense pleasure of being inside her again. She tossed her hair back, braced her hands on his chest. This was a woman who knew what she wanted, a woman who wasn't about to be denied. When she moved, her breasts tantalized him, beckoned him.

With his hands around her small waist, he took the nipple into his mouth while she took him on a slow, easy ride of pleasure that swamped him with sensations, an overpowering need, and a consuming hunger that would only be appeased by this woman.

Afterward with Summer in his arms again, he hand stroked her damp back. "You make me weak."

Her head lifted. Her hair tumbled around her bare shoulders. She'd never looked more desirable. "I don't think that was a compliment."

This time he couldn't resist tunneling his hand though her curly black hair, his eyes intense. "One day I'll leave."

"You're here now."

"You're stubborn."

"Answer one question?"

"What?"

"Would you rather it had been with another man?"

Hot rage filled him. His hand tightened. He lifted up, his arm going possessively around her, dragging her to him.

"I guess that answers my question. Looks like we're an item."

His hand flexed on her arm. "You make me forget to breathe at times, but this isn't forever."

The shadows were back in Sin's eyes. Something was bothering him. In the past few days they had been gone. She'd liked to think that she had helped push them away. She was half in love with him and falling fast. She'd give him her heart and the comfort of her body. He cared for her more than he would admit. She wouldn't be greedy and ask for more than he could give her.

"I'm where I want to be."

"What about C. J.?"

She lifted a brow at the mention of her cousin. "I'm a grown woman. I didn't interfere with him and Cicely, or all the other women before her."

"It's different for men."

"Only men think that way," she countered. "Let's try out your big bathtub, then if you have enough strength afterward, I'll cook you breakfast."

He brushed her hair from her face. "I don't think there's much in the refrigerator."

She looked at him through a sweep of her lashes. "I asked my team to bring over a few things."

"You knew this would happen?" he asked, not sure how he felt about it.

She kept his gaze. "You need to eat better. I was hoping for a chance to be the one who took care of you, but I admit I wanted you to notice me as a woman, for you to stop avoiding me."

"I was trying to be noble."

"Sin, you say you don't want me hurt. How do you think I'll feel if you send me home now?"

He didn't have to think long. "Used," he said tightly.

"Exactly. So letting me stay is the best alternative—plus the fringe benefits are incredible." She kissed him on the lips. "I'm old enough to know what I want, and intelligent enough to know that one day one of us will want to move on, but until that time, why can't we just be happy and enjoy the time we have?"

"You seem to have thought a lot about this."

"My feelings for you started changing a couple of months ago," she told him truthfully. "I've probably had longer to think about this."

"I wish things were as simple as you want to believe," he said, obviously troubled.

Her eyes narrowed, then she rolled out of bed, glanced around, then picked up her blouse, jeans, boots. "Sin, I want to be with you. I'm not afraid of the risks. We've had fun as friends, it could be even better as lovers. That's a decision you have to make." Her chin lifted. "You should know that if I walk out the door, it won't be so easy to get me to walk back through. You'll have to fight for me. For us."

He came off the bed in a controlled rush. "Are you threatening me?"

"No, I'm telling you as plain as I know that while I give freely, if it's tossed back in my face, I won't be so foolish as to do so again." She swallowed and started for the door.

Everything within him wanted to call her back. Closing his eyes, he locked his knees and fisted his hands. The quiet sound of the door closing had his eyes snapping open.

She was gone.

Summer swallowed and fought tears, fought the urge to go back inside and take Sin on any terms.

She couldn't. She'd dreamed of this day too long. She wanted the man she first gave her body to to want her as fiercely as she wanted him, to be as sure as she was.

Sin had doubts.

The intimacy had been beautiful, unbelievable, but they couldn't spend all of their time in bed. There had to be more to keep them together than physical attraction. Although that was pretty incredible.

She had to admit that, once she'd gotten over her crush, she'd never expected Sin to be that man, until her feelings started to change. Sin might want her, but apparently not enough.

Loneliness overwhelmed him. Summer was gone.

The woman he treasured above all others was gone from his life forever. He had given up so much because of something he had no control over. The day his father had been diagnosed had forever changed and shaped his life.

Now it had taken the only person in the world who could banish those days when everything seemed to close in around him, the days that life seemed hopeless. He turned toward the bed and saw the white swatch of lace by the foot of the bed where he'd tossed it last night.

Picking up the bra, he crushed the delicate fabric in his hand. It was all he had left.

Only if you let it be.

Sin heard Alex's words as clearly as if he'd been standing there. Sin glanced at the bra spilling over his fisted hand. He hadn't achieved his success by looking at the odds, but by disregarding them. He went all-out for what he wanted.

Fight for me. For us.

Sin raced for the door and jerked it open only to pull up short. Summer stood there in her untucked white blouse and jeans. Her boots in her hand.

Surprise flashed across her face. Her gaze swept down his naked body. She swallowed and reached for the bra in his hand. Sin held it out of the way.

"That's mine."

"Possession is nine-tenths of the law, I believe."

Summer folded her arms. "You want to discuss law when you're naked."

"You could take off that blouse and jeans so you'd be naked as well," he said and watched her eyes jerk to his, her arms slowly unfold. "I've never felt as lonely or as miserable as when you closed that door. You center my life. With you, the impossible becomes possible. I don't want you to go."

"I suppose this is where I forgive you and we have makeup sex?" she asked, not moving, her facial expression unchanged.

"I certainly hope so, or we could go out," he said, willing to do whatever it took now that he'd stopped fighting his feelings and wanted Summer for as long as God allowed.

She brushed by him to enter the bedroom. "I can't leave without my underwear on."

The vise around his chest eased. He closed the door. "Where do you think we should look first?"

She dropped her boots. "The bed seems a logical place." She stood by the bed they'd wrecked and looked seductively over her shoulder at him. "Are you going to help?"

"I'm on it. Why don't I help you with those clothes so you can put everything on at the same time." He crossed to her, his legs steadier with each step. He hadn't lost her. He still had time.

He stopped when nothing separated them but her

clothes, then circled his arms around her waist and just held on. Her arms circled his as she leaned back against him.

"As long as you need and want me, I'll be here," she whispered softly.

He swallowed, his hold tightened. No questions. No recrimination. But then, hadn't she always been there for him, just as he'd been there for her?

His head angled. Brushing his lips against her neck, he felt her shiver. Delicate, responsive, and his. He wasn't going to waste any more time worrying about what might happen; he was going to enjoy being with the one woman he didn't want to live without.

His hands slipped the buttons of her blouse free. He pulled it off and unbuttoned her jeans. Bending, he tugged her jeans over her long legs, taking his time enjoying seeing her body slowly revealed, the slight trembling when he brushed his lips against the back of her knees, nipped her thigh.

Standing, he drew her into his arms. "Thank you."

She kissed him on the shoulder. "I figure you'd make it worth my while."

Chuckling, he tumbled them into bed, covering her body with his as his lips fastened on hers. He planned to do that and much, much more.

Dressed in his white shirt with the sleeves rolled up, and as playful and as beautiful as he'd ever seen her, Summer prepared their breakfast. Sin took immense satisfaction that he had put that look on her face.

He thought about Dianne's comment about wishing she had mementos of her dates with Alex before they were engaged, and wondered if he could get away with keeping Summer's bra. Probably not. She might not have any inhibitions when they were making love, but otherwise it was a different story. Luckily for him she hadn't wanted to leave her bra and panties, and had dressed in her jeans and blouse and stood outside his door trying to decide what to do.

Maybe she wouldn't miss one of the ivory combs she'd used to pin up her hair when they were in his Jacuzzi. It was certainly worth a shot. She was the only woman he was ever going to allow in his life, and when the day came that he had to leave, he wanted to have something of hers to keep forever.

"What?"

He got off the stool and went to her. Just looking at her made his heart sing. "You look good in that shirt."

"Another fantasy of mine. I have an active imagination."

"So I'm learning." He grinned and skimmed his hands from her thighs up to her waist. Too bad she'd insisted on wearing the panties they'd found in the bed, but there were only a couple of buttons fastened on the shirt, so he got a tantalizing view of her luscious breasts if she moved a certain way. He'd never appreciated his shirt more.

"Have a seat before I burn these," she said, her voice shaky.

"I'd eat them anyway," he said, but he took his seat. He watched her work and wanted to do something to please her. "What do you say we fly up to East Hampton for a picnic?"

"The Yankees are playing today," she reminded him.

"I'd rather be with you," he said, meaning every word. Before now he would have thought it sacrilege to miss one of their games.

Obviously touched, she swallowed, swallowed again, and then slid the perfectly cooked omelet onto a plate. "I can think of only one thing I'd like to do better."

His eyes darkened with desire. "We'll do both."

Hand in hand Summer and Sin walked on the pristine beach of East Hampton. The calm blue waters of the ocean lapped against the shore. Seagulls screamed and dove for food. The wind tugged at her unbound hair. In the distance, she could see a blue-and-white windmill. In her hand she carried her sandals. She had a goofy grin on her face and didn't care. She couldn't ever remember being this happy, and it was all because of the incredible man next to her.

"Anyplace look good for us to stop?" Sin asked.

Summer glanced around. Couples were sunning, women reading, children building sand castles. She'd wanted the impossible, a secluded place where they could eat the picnic lunch Sin had ordered and get in some more kissing. There were definitely fewer people in this area, but it wasn't the isolation she sought.

"Everyone is having too much fun to notice me kissing you." To prove his point, he dropped a kiss on her lips. "See."

Summer curved her arm around his neck. "You call that a kiss?"

His free hand curved around her waist. "Without leading to something that will get us arrested, yes."

Grinning, she kissed him on the lips. "It's a good thing I have plans for you or I might just chance it."

His eyes darkened. "Summer."

The smile slid from her face. He said her name with such reverence and need. "I didn't know a touch could make you want this badly."

"Neither did I." A breath shuddered over his beautifully shaped lips, lips that she distinctly remembered sliding hungrily over her body. She couldn't wait to feel them again. He stepped back. "Please pick a spot. I'm not sure I can walk much farther."

Summer frowned up at Sin. His body was in top shape. She had seen every glorious inch of it. She— Her gaze slanted downward and saw the unmistakable bulge in his swim trunks when his open shirt flapped in the wind. She licked her lips.

"Summer, that's not helping."

Her head jerked up. She knew what would. "I wish we were alone."

"I wanted to give you this," he said simply.

She reached for the basket in his hand, pulled the blanket from his shoulder. They'd shared so much on this beach. "Go take a dip. I'll find a spot then join you."

"And make it better and worse." Dropping a kiss on her temple, Sin started for the water.

Summer watched him, admiring the athletic grace, the sleek muscles, the long legs. He was gorgeous, sexy, and, for the time being, all hers. A moment of sadness hit her before she pushed it away. She wasn't going to worry about Sin one day walking away. He hadn't entered into their affair lightly. He wasn't about to leave anytime soon.

Placing the basket on the sand, she spread out the blanket then placed the basket, towels, and her shoes on top. She caught sight of Sin's powerful arms as he cut through the water, remembered those same arms and hands holding her, loving her so completely. She felt the quickening in her lower body. She wanted him again. She also wanted Sin not to have any regrets about them being together. Pulling off her cover-up, she tossed it on top of the towels and walked toward Sin.

Sin saw Summer coming toward him and swam toward the beach. His body hardened even more. The black bikini triangle top and side-tie string bottom had his hands aching to remove the pieces of cloth, his heart beating like a jackhammer. Temptation was a woman named Summer. He swam toward the beach, then stood. The water lapped around his hips.

Wind tossed her beautiful hair. She didn't seem to notice. Her eyes were fastened on him. Even from a distance he saw the burning desire in her eyes, the same desire he knew blazed within him. He burned for her. She was all that he desired and thought he'd never have.

She kept coming until she stood in front of him. "I figure there's only one way to get us though this."

"Yeah."

"Yeah." Leaning over, she playfully splashed water in his face. He was so surprised he just stood there as she went farther into the water, then began swimming. "Bet you can't catch me."

He caught her before she had gone fifteen feet, his arm going around her waist. She squealed, laughed. His laughter joined her. "That was sneaky."

"It got you to laugh," she said, grinning at him. "I like hearing you laugh."

He brushed his hand over her face. "Laughing was always easy with you."

"The same here. You helped me become the woman I am today." She grinned. "Who better to enjoy the benefits?"

Laughter spilled from his lips as he pulled her

closer. Only Summer would say anything so out-
landish, and he was going to take her up on her generous offer.

He didn't want her to go.

It was selfish, he admitted to himself as Summer
handed him a stuffed garment bag with the clothes
she'd selected to change into before the restaurant
opened. He wasn't ready to let her out of his sight.

They'd arrived back at her apartment from the
beach almost two hours ago, taken another shower
together, and fallen into bed. He couldn't get enough
of her. The loving was sweet, wild, passionate. He
liked holding her, looking at her.

The crystal clock on her beside chest read 6:32
PM. Radcliffe's opened at five. She'd been late before, but she'd never missed going in. Silently he
reached for the bag in her hand she said contained
her shoes and accessories.

"You know I wouldn't go if I didn't have to."

He kissed her furrowed brow. "And here I thought
I had my poker face on."

Her hand cupped his cheek. "It's because I saw
the same misery in my face when I was putting on
my makeup."

"The car is waiting."

She caught his arm when he turned away. "If you
want me to stay, I will."

He simply stared. Radcliffe's was so much more
than a restaurant: it was the fulfillment of a dream,

her baby, her creation. "Thank you, but you're going to work. I can work on the paperwork I couldn't concentrate on yesterday."

"You want to come in and have dinner?" she asked, a bit hesitant.

"If you don't want people to know about us, I understand." This was new to her, but he didn't want to hide their relationship. He'd handle C. J. when the time came.

She started out of the bedroom in a one-shoulder blue tie-dyed silk dress that he promised himself he was going to have the pleasure of slowly removing later on, then whipped back around. "It's not that. Am—am I going to see you when I close the restaurant? I know it's late . . ." Her voice trailed off.

The question caught him by surprise. "Come here." He waited until she was mere inches from him. He'd never seen an unsure Summer. "If I wouldn't make you later I'd put these things down and show you how much I'm going to miss you. I'll be there when you close and every night I'm in town, waiting for you when I should let you go home and rest."

Her eyes flickered close, but not before he saw the relief in them. She circled his waist and leaned into him. "I've been going home and resting for four years. I want to be with you."

He rubbed his bearded cheek against her silken hair that thirty minutes ago had trailed across his chest, then lower. His body clenched at the erotic memory. "I have a surprise for you. Do you mind if we stop at my place before I take you home after the restaurant closes?"

She straightened, her eyes wide. "A surprise. For me? What is it? No, don't tell me."

"Good, because I wasn't going to."

She playfully swatted him with her hand, then brushed her lips across his. "I bet I could get it out of you."

His breath hitched. "You're probably right, but you'd be late and I wouldn't have the enjoyment of seeing your expression later on."

"In that case . . ." She started for the front door. "I expect to be wowed in *all* areas."

Shaking his head he started after her. "I'll do my best."

Chapter 11

During the evening at Radcliffe's, Summer had thought occasionally about the surprise Sin had for her, but didn't have the slightest idea what it might be. Not even when he'd dropped by to dine had he given her any hint. What excited her most of all was knowing Sin wanted to spend as much time with her as she did with him.

He was waiting for her when she locked the front door of Radcliffe's. He'd spoken to the two bartenders who always waited until she was safely in a cab, then opened the back door of the limo.

"Ready for your surprise?"

"More than ready," she answered and climbed inside.

As soon as he was settled he reached for her hand. Summer leaned her head on his shoulder and sighed with contentment.

"Perhaps I should take you home."

She snuggled closer. "You do and you'll never dine at Radcliffe's again—among missing other pleasurable things."

From the shaking of his body, she knew he was laughing. "My place it is."

"Wise decision."

In less than fifteen minutes Sin opened his penthouse door. Summer let out a soft gasp. The terrace was bathed in white lights.

"We never had our dance."

Still holding her hand, he crossed to the terrace door and stepped out under the twinkling canopy of lights. Tiny white lights circled the topiary. Flameless candles flickered on the lip of the walled waterfall. Faintly, she heard the pounding surf of the ocean. Except for the recorded sounds of the ocean, his terrace was almost an exact duplicate of the night of the party. "How?"

He kissed her on the forehead and drew her into her arms. "You aren't supposed to ask how, just enjoy."

Squeezing her eyes tight to fight the sudden stinging, she curved her arms around his waist. Her surprise had taken a lot of time, talent, and effort. More than that, it had taken thought and care.

No matter what he said, he cared. That was precious and priceless. "I . . ." She swallowed. "I've never had a better surprise."

"If you cry I'm unplugging every light," he warned, kissing her on the top of her head as he held her closer.

"Then kiss me so I won't."

His mouth found hers, brushing across her waiting lips. Reluctantly he lifted his head while he still had the willpower to do so. With a punch of the controls in his hand, the music changed to a slow instrumental. With a contented sigh, Summer leaned into Sin. "This is nice."

He kissed her hair. He couldn't help it. She made life so much more. Usually they liked to fast-dance, but tonight called for slow and dreamy under soft lights with the half-moon overhead.

"Your Yankees won today."

"So did I."

Laughing, she lifted her head. "We both did."

"I couldn't agree more." He rubbed his cheek against hers, sighed with the rightness of her here with him. The slow hum of the music sank into him as much as the woman in his arms.

His hand stroked up and down her elegant back, and he brushed his lips across her one bare shoulder. "You look stunning in this dress, but I promised myself that I'd take it off tonight."

Her head lifted, her eyes filled with sensual warmth. "And you're a man of your word."

With a push of a button the lights in the inner perimeter dimmed, leaving them in a warm glow on the topiary with the moon overhead. The music changed back to the sounds of the pounding surf of the ocean.

"Ah, beautiful," she sighed.

Grasping the tab of the zipper in the back of her dress, he drew it down, then stepped back and let the dress slither down her body. She wore light blue lace underwear and a garter belt that made his mind fuzz. His mouth dried. She made his body crave. He reached for her and she stepped just out of reach.

"I get to undress you this time." She shoved off his jacket, unbuttoned his shirt and tossed it aside. Next came his belt.

"Is this another fantasy?" he asked, determined to maintain control.

"Yes." She unzipped his pants, then bent to pull them and his shorts down. She paused as his erection sprang free. She leaned her head forward. His hand stopped her. "No." It was a guttural sound of warning. He swallowed hard.

She looked up at him with determined eyes. "Before the night is over, I will."

His body clenched and trembled as she continued to pull his pants down; then he heard her mutter. He glanced down.

"I forgot to take off your shoes. Lift up your foot." She slipped off his loafers. "Some seductress I am."

Before she could stand, he scooped her into his arms and headed for the nearest cushioned backless settee. "I've never trembled with need, never wanted this badly. I don't want a practiced woman. I only want you."

Her shaking hand cupped his cheek. "I only want you."

Pleased beyond words, he placed her on the settee, then followed her down, his body covering hers. "You're all I want."

"Then show me."

His mouth fitted to hers, hot and hungry, as his greedy hands roamed over her body, teasing, tantalizing. He moved downward, brushing his lips across her quivering stomach, his teeth nipping at the flesh just above the garter belt.

Her hands clutched at his head as he seduced her, loved her, made her burn and squirm beneath him. Her last coherent thought was that Sin had wowed her in all areas and then some.

He'd never felt so content. With all the lights off and Summer wrapped in his arms, they stared up at the moon overhead. He didn't spend the night with women, and they certainly didn't spend the night in his place. Summer had changed all that. "I might have done something to annoy you. I dismissed the driver until nine tomorrow."

Her head slowly lifted from his chest. "I have a change of clothes in my bag for work tomorrow."

"You bring a nightgown?"

"I figured I wouldn't need one."

"Smart woman." He rolled on top of her.

Sin exited the limo first the next morning, then helped Summer out. It was 10:07 AM. They'd kept the driver waiting for over forty minutes while Sin showed her how wickedly talented his mouth and hands were.

"Have a great day," she told him, still in a bit of a sensual haze. If she closed her eyes she knew she'd feel him moving against her, the hot pleasure of him.

"It certainly started that way." Grinning, ignoring her blush, he pulled her into his arms and kissed her until her toes curled in her Prada flats. Then he got back into the car.

Summer stared as the car merged with the traffic. The man could kiss, but he did everything well and she benefited immensely. She turned to enter the restaurant and saw Joan and Karen, their mouths gaped, their eyes enormous.

Summer grinned, hoped it wasn't smug, and continued to her office. When Sin had stopped by the restaurant the night before for dinner, they'd kept it cool. Looked like he didn't plan on keeping their affair a secret, and that was fine by her. She'd no more settled in her chair when there was a tentative knock on her door.

"Come in." She wasn't surprised to see Joan and Karen. However, she was surprised to see the frowns, their nervousness. Both women were usually happy and carefree. "What is it?"

"Summer, we didn't know Sin was yours," Joan blurted.

"Yeah, we didn't know." Karen bit her lower lip. "We wouldn't have said those things."

Summer realized they were scared she might take offense about their saying they were interested in him. "I wasn't seeing him then, and even though I am now, I don't expect women not to notice how gorgeous he is." Crossing her arms, she leaned back in her chair. "Anything more, though, and I'd have to hurt you."

Sin was whistling when he entered his office Monday morning. Going to his desk, he saw Michael and his family's picture and the sound died. *Please be all right.* Sin picked up the phone and dialed.

"Hey, Payton. How did the party go?" Michael asked in his usual cheerful manner.

"Fantastic." Sin's smile returned as he leaned back in his chair. "Summer did a fantastic job."

"You sound mighty happy."

"I am," Sin said. *Then and later.* His grin widened. "I'm going over the contract Sun Beverages sent me for Cameron. I should be through with it in a few days."

"Take your time. We want to make sure it's everything you negotiated so hard for."

Sin relaxed even more. Michel sounded fine.

"Nancy just buzzed me," Michael said. "Staff meeting in five. I'll call you back and we can go over this week's schedule."

"Will do. Bye." Sin disconnected the call, then punched in Summer's office.

"Hi. I miss you," she said.

"I miss you more," he said, leaning his head forward and groaning. "I can't believe I said that."

Summer laughed. "It's a good thing I'm not the sensitive type."

He palmed his forehead. "Summer, I'm sorry. That didn't come out right."

"I think it came out exactly right," she said. "Do you have any plans for dinner?"

"I was hoping you'd take pity on me and invite me to Radcliffe's."

"How about a five-course dinner in my office around ten? You get two glasses of wine."

"I accept the offer, and the wine limitation, although we both know I have a high tolerance for alcohol."

"Yes, we do, but I want you extremely wide awake and fully functional when you take me home. See you at ten."

Sin blinked, than laughed. Summer was proving a surprising, delightful woman. He couldn't wait to see her and show her just how functional he could be, but first he had to make an important phone call.

Less than two hours later Summer simply stared at the enormous flower arrangement of orchids, canna lilies, and birds-of-paradise on her desk. The crystal Waterford vase was exquisite.

"That's one man who knows how to make a statement," Daphne said.

"That's not all I bet he—"

Summer didn't look around to see if Kerri, Daphne, or Joan had stopped Karen from speaking. Summer's grin would have said it all. The four women had followed the delivery guy into her office.

"Ah, sorry, Summer," Karen said. "I forgot."

"Easy to do when the man is Sin." Summer leaned over, inhaled the soft scent, then plucked the card.

I miss you.
       Sin

Summer rounded the desk and picked up the phone. She opened her mouth to ask the women to excuse her, but they were already heading out the door. She dialed Sin's number. His secretary put her though immediately.

"They're exquisite." She fingered an orchid petal. "Thank you."

"I'm glad you liked them."

"*Like* is a mild word. We'll eat in my office."

"Perfect. That way I can nibble on you as well."

Her heart thumped. "And I can return the favor. Good-bye, Sin."

"Bye, Summer, and don't be surprised if I'm a bit early."

"Then come when you can. I'm sure we can find something to do in my office."

He chuckled. "Stop tempting me. Take care."

"I will. Bye." Summer hung up the phone, sighed,

then headed for the kitchen. She knew exactly what she wanted Kerri to prepare for their meal.

Sin arrived at Radcliffe's shortly after nine. The hostess grinned and waved him to the back. He didn't miss the brief knowing looks from the waitresses, the warning ones from the men. They cared. Summer was easy to love. The word didn't scare him as much as it would have before Sunday morning when they'd first made love.

Summer was a precious gift and he was going to treasure her. He knocked on her door.

"Come in."

Opening the door, he stepped inside her office and came to a complete halt. His breath hitched.

"Hi, Sin. I see you're early." She nodded toward the door. "You might want to close that."

He did without taking his eyes from her. He couldn't if his life had depended on it. Summer, in a sinful excuse for a gown, stood under the small chandelier in the middle of her office. The silk gold dress made her skin glow and stopped midthigh. Embellished with flowers over gossamer, barely there fabric, the gown made his imagination run wild.

"That's some dress," he said when he could get his brain to work.

"I wanted to wear this the night of your party." She went to the table for two draped with a white tablecloth and two place settings and lit the tall white candles.

"I would have been a whimpering mess."

Blowing out the match, she came to him and looped both arms around his neck. Her warm scent of jasmine wrapped around him and tugged. "Daphne is going to take care of everything so we won't be disturbed."

He glanced at the table. He'd called to tell her he was on his way. There was only bread and butter there. "You're going out in the restaurant in that dress?"

She chuckled, seductive and teasing, causing his body to clench and his hands to tighten possessively around her waist.

"Summer?"

She brushed her lips against his. "Karen is going to deliver the courses when I call. Only you'll see me in this dress."

He breathed a little easier before a thought struck. "Then why did you buy it?"

"Guess," she purred.

To please and tempt me. And he couldn't be more thrilled. He was well and truly hooked, so he took it like a man and kissed her.

"Your monthly pool game night is tomorrow night," Summer said as she lay in Sin's arms Tuesday night. He'd insisted on bringing her home. She'd insisted he stay. They both had gotten what they wanted.

He kissed her on the forehead. Moonlight shone

though her double windows. They'd been together every night since his party. "You nervous?"

"I didn't think I would be." She braced herself on her elbow to stare down at him. She loved just looking at him. Loved him. "They all probably know about us. I'm not ashamed of being with you."

Sin brushed her hair aside, letting the silky tendrils drift through his hand. "You just don't want C. J. to think differently about you."

"Or take a swing at you," she said, biting her lip. "Thinking and knowing we're together are two different things. C. J. appointed himself my guardian long before I lost my parents."

"I'm glad he was there to keep you safe and scare off all the other boys and men before I saw what was before my eyes."

She brushed her lips against his. "Flattery."

"Truth." His stared at her intently. "C. J. is my oldest friend. I admire and respect him, would do anything for him, but giving you up isn't an option." Michael hadn't had any more episodes. Maybe Sin was wrong. Maybe he could have a life of happiness.

Summer threw one leg over him, straddling him, then leaned down until their lips almost touched. "Same goes for me. Giving you up isn't an option."

Her warmth and slight weight felt so right against him. This would work out. It had to, and he was going to make sure that it did.

* * *

Sin purposefully arrived early Wednesday night at Callahan's Bar. He wanted to talk with C. J. before Summer arrived—if she could get away. She worked harder than anyone he knew, never complaining, helping her friends no matter what the cost to herself. She deserved the best life had to offer. And while they were together, he was going to do everything in his power to see that it happened.

Opening the door to the bar, Sin waved to Sam at the bar and continued to the back booth. He was almost there when he saw C. J. with one arm wrapped around Cicely; each had a pool cue, both grinning at the other. It was a sight Sin never thought he'd see, playboy C. J. as deep in love as you could get.

It just reaffirmed that sometimes unexpected happiness tapped you on the shoulder. He hung on to that. He had to. Maybe, just maybe, things would turn out all right for Michael and him.

"Should I ask who is winning?" From the number of balls on the table, one of them was losing. Badly.

Still grinning, Cicely said, "Hi, Sin. Need you ask?"

"She's using an unfair advantage every time she bends over to play," C. J. said. "It breaks my concentration."

"Some people will use any excuse." Cicely bent over with the pool cue to line up a shot.

"Not from where I'm standing." C. J. stared at her butt encased in slacks.

Cicely pocketed two balls, then quickly moved around the table to sink two more, then the eight-ball in the side pocket. She straightened. "Game over. I won. When we're married, your apartment will be our pied-à-terre, and my house will be our main residence."

C. J. shook his head. "Two out of three."

Cicely kissed him on the chin. "Nope. I've always wanted a pied-à-terre. It's sounds much more elegant than saying 'my second home.'"

"Since I'm the reason you're not in Paris, I guess I can go along with my place being our second home."

Cicely placed her cue stick on the table. "You're the reason I'm happier than I've even been. Paris would mean nothing without you in my life."

Knowing the kiss was coming, and not just a brush of lips, but one that made your body heat with desire, your heart thump with joy, Sin busied himself racking the balls. Four days ago, he wouldn't have had any idea what that kiss meant, how a woman could stand at the center of your life and you couldn't imagine her not being there.

"I'm going to collect my other prize. A hamburger and onion rings." Cicely patted Sin on the shoulder. "He's all yours."

"How did I get that lucky?" C. J. asked, staring after Cicely.

"It certainly wasn't clean living." Sin tossed the eight-ball in his hand.

"I could say the same thing about you." C. J. snatched the ball out of the air.

Sin met C. J.'s uncompromising gaze without flinching. They'd been friends since the eighth grade. Because both were strong-willed and hardheaded, they'd bumped heads more than a few times, but nothing major, and never over a woman. Still, Summer wasn't just any woman.

"No comment."

"Several actually." Sin plucked the ball from C. J.'s hand. "I didn't see this coming. Summer is everything I want in a friend, a woman I want to get to know better and so much more. She makes the day brighter, better. I just see her face, hear her laughter, and my problems fade."

"I'd think you were full of it if I didn't feel the same way about Cicely." C. J. put his hands on his hips. "Saturday night I wanted to rearrange your face until Alex talked to me."

Sin wasn't afraid Alex had betrayed a confidence. If he had, there was no way C. J. wouldn't have tried to break Sin and Summer up.

"He reminded me of the type of man you are, then I looked at Summer and knew it was too late. Choices had been made," C. J. finished.

There was one more thing. "Initially she said she didn't care what you thought about us being together, considering your past, but she loves and admires you, so she's a bit nervous about your reaction when you see each other again."

C. J. folded his arms and leaned against the pool table. His gaze was unflinching. "So you're here first."

"I'm here," Sin said. "Make her feel bad, treat her any differently, and I'll be in your face."

C. J.'s arms dropped to his sides. He straightened. "You threatening me?"

"Calm down, you two." Alex inserted himself between the two men.

"He started it," C. J. flung.

"If need be, I'll finish it," Sin said. "Hurt her at your own risk."

"Sin," Alex began, but he stopped when C. J. held up his hand.

"She means that much to you?"

"And more," Sin answered without hesitation. "She thinks the world of you. She cried for days when you left to go tramping around the world. You're the big brother she never had."

"Guys," Dianne said, joining them. "Summer just walked through the door. I don't think Cicely will be able to detain her for long."

"Hi, Summer," Cicely greeted, standing directly in her path.

"Hello, Cicely." Over her shoulder, Summer saw C. J. and Sin in the back by the pool table with Alex and Dianne. None of them was smiling.

"Want a burger?" Cicely asked. "Let's go to the bar and order."

"No, thank you." With her longtime ease at side-stepping people, Summer went around Cicely and straight to the back of the bar. She stopped in front of C. J. "Say what's on your mind."

She felt Sin's hand catch hers. "He's fine with us, isn't that right, C. J.?"

"Of course he is," Cicely said. "How about we play partners tonight? Dianne and Alex can play Sin and Summer. We'll take the winner."

"I think not." C. J. stepped closer to Summer. "I'd say you grew up on me, but I've known that for a long time."

"Yes," Summer said softly. She wanted C. J.'s approval, but she wanted Sin more.

C. J. looked at Sin. "Do you know he actually threatened me if I hurt you? As if I ever would. When you walked through the door, I was just about to tell him nothing could ever change the way I feel about you, even if you have bad taste. I was hoping you'd get someone who looked as good as I do."

Summer's smile trembled. She reached out and took C. J.'s hand. "If I squint and the light is just right, he's not so bad."

C. J. grinned. "If you say so. In any case, I'll forgive him his bad manners in *my bar* since I know caring about a woman can mess with a man's thinking. I guess you know he has a big head."

"He has a bigger heart," Summer said softly, her warm gaze going to Sin.

"You seem to have found it," C. J. responded.

"Thank you." With one arm curved possessively around Summer's shoulders, a little abashed, Sin stuck out the other one to C. J. "Sorry. Guess I over-reacted."

The handshake was firm. "Accepted. We both know I've been there. Now let's go have a drink to celebrate the occasion, and the fact that *no one* has to go to the emergency room and see Dr. Cortes."

Chapter 12

Since C. J. and Cicely's engagement, Summer was becoming used to Cicely and Dianne meeting in her office to discuss wedding plans. She actually enjoyed the meeting and the women, enjoyed their growing friendship. Now that she and Sin were an official item, she understood so much more the looks that passed between her best friends. Loving a man was incredible. If she had to hide that fact from Sin, she wasn't bothered by it. He'd proved over and over he cared.

"I can't believe I have an appointment to look at wedding gowns in a couple of days." Cicely's trembling hand covered her quivering stomach. "With all the photo shoots and assignments I've done over the years, I've never been this nervous."

"It's understandable." Dianne reached across the small round table in Summer's office and grabbed Cicely's unsteady hand. "As I said, I almost drove Greg crazy when I was trying to decide on mine."

Cicely looked at Summer. "Are you sure you can meet us?"

Us was C. J's mother and Dianne. "As the maid of honor, I'd be hurt if you hadn't asked me."

Cicely nodded. "I know how hectic life can get when you're in a relationship, and although you're in town and not flying off to parts unknown, your hours are crazier than mine."

"We make it work," Summer said with a grin. "Sin takes good care of me."

"I'll bet." Dianne slapped her hands over her mouth.

Summer's grin widened. "Yes, he does, and I try to do the same thing with him." She was shameless with Sin and didn't care who knew it.

All of the women burst out laughing. Dianne said, "I hear you. Five months ago I was miserable. Now I wake up with Alex by my side and cherish each day with him."

"Two months ago I thought I wanted the editor-in-chief position at our Paris branch. Then I walked into Callahan's, and now I'm counting the days until we're married." Cicely fingered her diamond engagement ring.

Summer swallowed the sudden knot in her throat. "I'm happy for you."

"You love Sin, don't you?" Dianne asked softly.

"More than I thought possible." Summer bit her lower lip. "More each day."

"Give him time," Cicely said. "We all know how hard C. J. fought admitting he loved me. I fought just as hard."

Summer plucked a tissue from a box on her desk. "I promised myself I wouldn't be greedy. He—he told me this wasn't forever, that he wasn't the marrying kind."

Cicely stood and went to Summer. "Yet he was ready to take on C. J. on your behalf."

"He's always been protective of me." Summer shrugged. "It didn't mean anything special."

"Don't be so sure," Dianne told her. "When Sin looks at you—which is most of the time when you're in the same room—he has the intense, possessive look of a man who's looking at his greatest desire."

"Lust isn't love," Summer said, then frowned on seeing the smile that passed between Cicely and Dianne.

"I told Dianne the same thing when I was trying to explain what was going on between me and C. J.," Cicely confided.

"And look where she is now." Dianne held up Cicely's left hand.

Summer stared at the glittering stone. "I don't know if it's best to hope and be disappointed, or not hope at all."

"I think you do," Cicely said softly. "C. J. said you and Sin are alike in many ways. You're both fighters. You go after what you want and you don't quit until you have it. You don't know any other way. That was one of the reasons he was initially concerned about you. I probably shouldn't say this."

Summer caught her friend's hands. "You're not leaving my office until you do."

"C. J. said Sin is different around you. With other women, he couldn't care less. He's cordial, but they don't occupy his thoughts the way you do. Sin wants you to be happy and would go to any lengths to see that happen, including picking a fight with his oldest friend."

"Alex said the same thing," Dianne confided. "Sin cares about you, but it's your choice."

"Hope or fold?" Cicely asked.

"Fight," Summer answered and held up her hand for a high-five. "Now let's go join our men in the bar."

"Sinclair, I've been looking for you."

Sin turned around on his stool at the far end of Radcliffe's bar. He'd already recognized the angry voice of Glen Atkins. When Sin stood, he smelled the alcohol on the other's man breath, saw the anger in his eyes. "It's crowded in here. Why don't we go outside?"

The man's face hardened. "There you go, ordering me around again. I don't take orders from you, you take them from me."

Sin was a breath away from telling Glen how very wrong he was when he caught sight of Summer and saw the worry in her face. "Where would you like to talk?"

Glen rocked back on his heels and looked at the

two men behind him, who had the same bulky build. They were teammates of Glen. "Told you he'd heel like a puppy dog. I'm money in the bank. How'd you make out with Marsha at the ESPYs?" He laughed nastily. "How did it feel coming after a real man?"

Sin's hands flexed. Summer had heard every word. As bad as he wanted to smash in the jerk's face, he wasn't brawling in her restaurant.

"You can use my office," Summer offered.

Glen jerked around, his gaze tracking Summer from her head to her feet before coming back up to her breasts and staying there. "Well, hello."

Sin was moving before he knew it. Alex blocked his path. Sin started to shove him aside only to find C. J. in the way as well. "Get out of the way!" Sin snarled.

Glen faced Sin and held up his hands. "There's nothing between us but air and opportunity." He laughed derisively. "Let's get this over with." He spoke to Summer. "Where's your office? After I'm finished with him, maybe a hot number like you and I can—"

"I'll show you," C. J. interrupted. His voice tightly controlled, he met Glen's hard stare.

"Whatever." Glen and the two men with him started after C. J.

Summer caught Sin's arm. The muscles were like warm steel. "My chairs are irreplaceable. So are you."

"He stepped over a line," Sin said, his voice cold.

Summer palmed his face. "What he said doesn't matter."

"To me, it does." Removing her hands, he headed for her office.

Alex's hand closed on the doorknob, but he didn't open Summer's office door. "You let the rage you're feeling get the best of you and that loudmouth wins. You're smarter than that."

"I want to take him down," Sin said, fury surging though him. The bastard had insulted Summer.

"Then do it your way, and not his." Alex opened the door.

Glen straightened from leaning against the front of Summer's desk. "I thought you had rabbited."

"You were anxious to talk, so talk."

Glen snickered. "You're the big man now with these two duds."

"They're my friends. Unlike these two with you," Sin said. "They wouldn't be with you if you weren't trying to be the big man and letting it rain with money at strip clubs. When you're out of money you can ill afford to lose, they'd dump you like yesterday's garbage."

Glen moved quickly to stand in front of Sin. "You got a big mouth. Talking to my agent like I'm some kind of kid. I'm a grown man." He hooked a thumb to his chest. "I do what I want to do when I want."

Sin had heard all the big talk before. "Not if you want to remain my client."

Glen got in Sin's face. "You trying to bluff me? *Me.* Voted the MVP for three straight years. I don't need you to work a deal for me. My stats speak for themselves."

"Exactly," Sin said. "That last MVP was two years ago. You've dropped ten places this year alone. You're sinking like a stone and you only have yourself to blame."

The running back's face filled with rage. "So I've had a slow year. Everybody has them sooner or later. Once the season starts, I'm coming back stronger than ever."

Looking into Glen's face, Sin saw the fear the man was unable to hide. Even he didn't believe that lie. "If that's all you have to say, this conversation is over."

Glen caught Sin's arm when he turned to leave. "I say when it's over."

Sin stared from his arm to the man. "That's where you're wrong."

Laughing, Glen lifted both hands. "You wanna run up on me? I could mess you up with one hand behind my back."

Alex cleared his throat. "Do you think we should tell him Sin has a black belt?"

"Nope," C. J. said. "He insulted Summer, but if Sin breaks one of her chairs, he's in for it."

Glen tsked. "You trying to frighten me?"

"Stating fact." Alex glanced at his watch. "The women aren't going to stay out much longer."

"Playtime's over, fellows," C. J. told them, unfolding his arms and straightening.

"Like any of you chumps are gonna make us leave," Glen sneered.

"Walking or being carried." Sin said. "Your choice, but you're leaving."

"Well, since you're being so inhospitable—" Glen started past Sin, then pivoted and swung his fist toward Sin's face.

Sin threw up his arm, blocking the blow, then came up with the heel of his other hand to hit Glen directly on the nose. He hollered in pain. As Glen was falling backward, Sin kicked him in the chest, sending him crashing against the wall.

Whirling, Sin crouched, hands upraised, palms out for the other men. They hadn't moved—whether from surprise or because Alex and C. J. had moved in front of them, Sin didn't know or particularly care. He straightened. "Take him and leave."

The men rushed to Glen. Each grabbed an arm and headed for the door. Glen came to, shaking his head, his nose swollen and dripping blood on his thousand-dollar, custom-made jacket. "Y-you bastard! You're fired! I don't need you!"

"My lawyer will overnight my acceptance of your verbal decision to your agent and to you." Sin walked over and looked Glen in the eyes. "Don't ever insult a woman in my presence or get in my face again."

Opening the door, Sin saw two of the bartenders

with the three women. "Show them out the back way," he instructed.

The women rushed inside and to their men. "We heard the crash, but Will and Steve wouldn't let us come in." Summer's worried gaze ran over the men. "Are you all right?"

"Sin did all the work," C. J. said.

"I could shake you for scaring me," Summer said. "Why would you risk getting hurt?"

"I didn't mean to worry you, but he crossed a line and I knew I couldn't work with him again." His fingertips feathered over her lips. "I'm all right. Not a scratch."

"You had better be." *I'll find out later,* she mouthed.

Sin grinned and hugged her to him, looking forward to later.

Early the next morning the ring of his iPhone cut through Sin's lazy contentment. He frowned, felt Summer's warm, naked body next to his, and decided he might not tear a new one for whoever would dare call at—he angled his head to the bedside clock—5:13 AM.

"Sin. Phone."

He dropped a kiss on Summer's bare shoulder before getting out of bed, glad he'd left the beside lamp on dim so he could see Summer's face when he pulled her close and she came apart in his arms.

The ring came again and he crossed the room to

snatch up his jacket. With the phone in his hand, he activated it more to keep from waking Summer up fully than from any interest in the call. He stared at the smooth curve of her shoulder. He knew well what was beneath the sheet, and when he got this rude person off the phone, he was going to—

"Why is life so effing hard?" came his brother's angry, high-pitched voice. "Nothing I do pleases anyone. Nobody appreciates me."

Sin's hand on the phone tightened as his brother spewed a litany of profanity. "Michael, it's all right. Where are Liz and the boys?"

"Why the hell do you want to know about them? You always cared about them more than me."

This wasn't his loving brother talking. Michael loved his children, idolized his wife. Sin left the bedroom and headed for the phone in the great room. Halfway there, he heard a click in his phone. Someone was trying to call him. *Liz.* He just prayed she and the boys were safe. "I love you, Michael. I just need to talk to Liz."

"She locked herself in the bathroom." Michael began to sob. "You know I wouldn't hurt her or the boys. I love her, but nobody loves me."

Sin heard another click of the phone and his gut clenched. Michael had hung up. The click came again. He quickly accepted the call. "Liz."

"Payton, oh, Payton," Liz sobbed.

"Liz, are you and the boys all right?" There was nothing but sobs. "Liz, I know it's hard but you have to calm down so I can help. Are you and the boys all right?"

More sniffles, then, "Yes. When he started yelling and becoming more agitated, I got the boys and locked us in the master bathroom. I'm scared, Payton. I don't know what to do. Do you think . . ."

She couldn't say the words and Sin couldn't blame her. She didn't want to face the harsh reality that the man she knew and loved was changing, would never be the same again.

"I'm going to call Dr. Kearns." Sin returned to the bedroom with the phone between his shoulder and ear. "He can be there in five minutes. I want him there when the ambulance arrives."

"Michael hasn't seen our family doctor since the physical you require all the employees to have every year."

"I've been in contact with him since Michael's first episode. Dr. Kearns knows the family history." Sin shot his arm through his shirt. "You and the boys stay there until Dr. Kearns comes."

"I-I don't hear anything, perhaps it's all right." Sobs came again. "He said we didn't love him. That hurt, Payton, because I could tell he believed it."

Sin's head fell forward. He swallowed. "Stay there, honey. Promise me. If Michael hurt you or the boys, he'd never get over it. I'm going to call Dr. Kearns, then my pilot. I'll be there as soon as I can."

"Payton."

He didn't see his black socks and toed on his loafers. "Yes?"

"I'm so scared."

He swallowed again. "So am I, but we're going to get the through this. I'm on my way."

"Hurry." The line went dead.

Sin grabbed his jacket and walked out of the bedroom without looking at the bed. He wanted too badly to hold Summer in his arms one last time. That was impossible now.

His first call was to Dr. Kearns, then his pilot. "I need to go to Dallas immediately. I'll meet you at the hangar." He shoved the phone in his pocket and started for the door.

"Is there is anything I can do?"

He jerked around before he could help himself. Dressed in his T-shirt that she liked to wear, she came toward him from the bedroom. How much had she heard? "No."

"When will you be back?"

"I won't. It's over." He walked out of the apartment without looking back.

Summer flinched when the door closed. She sensed the finality in Sin's voice. Beneath the harsh words there had been fear. She'd never heard him sound so . . . hopeless.

She returned to her bedroom and sat on the bed. Absently she picked up the pillow by her and wrapped both arms around it. No matter where they ended up in bed before going to sleep, Sin always ended up closer to the door. He'd joked about it, saying the reason was because she hogged the bed.

She knew it was because he was protecting her, the same way he always walked nearer the street. Sin took care of those he cared about.

His abrupt departure had something to do with his brother. She hadn't meant to listen, but the phone had woken her. The pain in his voice made her ache for him and his brother's family.

From the bits of conversation she'd heard about being safe, she wondered if Sin's brother abused his family, then dismissed the idea. Sin was proud of Michael and his family. Brother or not, Sin wouldn't have allowed Michael to run his Dallas office if he abused women.

So what was the reason he had abruptly left? The reason he'd gone from a passionate, playful lover in less than three hours to a man fighting pain and shadows? A man who now wanted no part of her.

She winced, hugged the pillow, smelled Sin's cologne. She'd give him the space he obviously wanted, but she wasn't going to give him up.

"Be safe, my darling."

Sin's jet touched down at Addison Airport outside Dallas, Texas, at a quarter past eight. He was out of his seat as soon as the engine shut down. When the door opened, he hurried down the steps. The limousine he'd ordered en route was waiting, the driver holding the back door open. Nodding briskly, Sin almost dove into the backseat and pulled out his phone again. His call was answered on the second ring.

"You're on the ground?" Liz asked.

"Yes. I'm leaving Addison Airport now," Sin answered. "With morning traffic, it will be thirty to forty minutes before I get there."

"Michael is still sleeping from the sedative Dr. Kearns gave him." Liz sounded tired—and who could blame her. Michael had handled going for a "drive" with Dr. Kearns, but had become agitated once they arrived at the hospital and had to be physically restrained. "I sent the boys down for breakfast."

"I'll sit with him when I get there so you can take a break, go get something to eat or go home."

"I can't leave him until he wakes up. I have to try and explain that this is for his benefit." The sobs came again. "What benefit? He'll only get worse if you're right. I'll lose my husband and best friend, the boys will lose their father."

Sin didn't know what to say. She was right. She was in an untenable position. There would be no winners, only losers. "I'll be there soon."

Summer didn't even try to go back to sleep. She'd sat on the side of the bed in Sin's T-shirt staring at the phone, hoping, praying he'd change his mind and call her.

He hadn't. She had been the one to call and leave messages—always the same. *Please call me.*

She'd wanted so badly to say *I love you,* but she honestly didn't know if that would hurt or help what he was going through. She might not know much about relationships, but she did know Sin cared about her.

She was still sitting on the bed when the first rays of sun stuck her bedroom window. She could sit there and be miserable, or she could try to find out why Sin had left so abruptly, then help him with whatever he was dealing with. Only two people she could think of might know what was going on. C. J. and Alex.

If Sin had told them in confidence what he was dealing with, neither would tell her. But she had to know he was all right. She'd never seen anyone look so desolate, so hopeless.

Throwing off Sin's T-shirt, she showered, dressed, and went downstairs to get a cab. She stepped out of the cab in front of Cicely's brownstone a few minutes before eight. When Cicely was in town and didn't have an early-morning assignment, C. J. took her to work then went on to Callahan Software. They had a crazy schedule, but love and respect for the other's profession was making it work.

Going up the steps, she rang the doorbell, then rang again.

C. J. opened the door wearing only dress slacks, the hard frown on his face disappearing in an instant. "Summer, what's the matter? Are you all right?"

It took several tries for her to get the words out. By the time she did, Cicely was there in a short robe. "Can I come in?

C. J. and Cicely reached for her at the same time. C. J. led Summer to a seat in the living room while Cicely went to the kitchen.

"It's too early for whiskey and there's no tea." C. J. knelt in front of her and held out the glass of orange juice Cicely handed him. "Drink and then you can tell me if I need to go to Sin's place and rearrange all of his body parts."

Summer's hands closed around the ice-cold glass. C. J. didn't know any more than she did. For some odd reason, she felt if she told him what had happened, she'd be the one betraying a confidence. "He had to leave this morning, unexpectantly. I guess I'm just feeling a little melancholy."

C. J. blinked hard. "What? You had me—"

"C. J.," Cicely said quietly.

C. J. pushed to his feet. "Don't mind me. My brain is mush from looking at plates and flatware patterns last night."

"Neither one of us has plates or flatware for a formal dinner. Your parents and friends will not come over and be served with a mismatched set," Cicely told him.

"Not even married, and she's reading me the riot act." He kissed Cicely on the cheek. "I'll go start breakfast." Halfway out of the room, he stopped. "Summer, you've never been flighty or the melancholy type. Since I know what it is to hit a rough spot when you're trying to find your way in a relationship, I'll *try* to stay out of it."

"Do you want to talk about it?" Cicely asked as soon as C. J. was no longer visible.

"Thanks, no." Summer placed the orange juice on a coaster and stood. "If C. J. hears from Sin, could you please call me?"

"Of course." Cicely walked with Summer to the door. "Sin didn't say how long he'd be gone?"

I'm not coming back. Summer bit her lower lip.

Cicely ran her hand up and down Summer's arm. "Love isn't easy, is it?"

"No."

"Take it from me, it's worth all of the uncertainty and tears."

"But you got your man."

"My money is on you that you will as well."

Chapter 13

Sin stepped off the elevator on the hospital's neurological floor and saw his nephews leaning against the wall. Their world had been turned upside down. He knew just what they were going through.

He easily remembered himself and Michael, scared and helpless, standing outside the hospital room of their father. There had been so many doctors and hospital visits, but their father's condition worsened instead of improving. He lost his job, alienated his friends and family until he in no way physically or emotionally resembled the hardworking and loving man they knew as husband, father, and friend.

The younger twin, Jardon, saw Sin and straightened. From twenty feet away, Sin saw the sheen of tears in his eyes. Sin's own throat tightened. He felt the weight of the whole damn mess rest squarely on his shoulders as he'd always known it would if Michael became ill.

The twins started toward him. For a split second,

Sin wanted to turn around and get back on the elevator. Anything but stand there, because he knew the questions they were going to ask, the lies he had to tell them.

But first, his arms went around both of them. Or at least tried. Michel had always said both sons would play football and now they did, as defensive linebackers. At sixteen, they weighed close to 180 and were five foot eleven in their stocking feet.

"I'm here, fellows, I'm here."

Jadon, the older by two and a half minutes, lifted his head. His eyes were red. "Mom's with Dad now. She said we couldn't go in yet."

"The doctor that came to the house last night is in there with another doctor. NEUROLOGIST was written on his lab coat." Jardon brushed his hand across his damp cheek. "Do you think Dad has a tumor? Is that why he's acting so strange?"

Sin clasped both nephews on the shoulder and told them what he was sure would be the first of many lies. "I don't know. Let me go in."

"They cut out tumors now and people are all right," Jadon stated. "Dad's going to be all right, isn't he, Uncle Payton?"

"Yes." Perhaps giving them false hope was wrong; he didn't know. He did know it was their mother's responsibility to tell them the truth, just as it had been his and Michael's mother's. How terrible for a mother to tell her sons that through no fault of their own, their bodies might carry a mutant gene that would kill them—but first it would make their lives a living hell.

Squeezing their shoulders one last time, Sin walked down the hall and entered the hospital room. He saw Michael immediately. He looked as scared as Sin and the rest of the family.

"Don't you say I have it. Don't you dare." Michael jerked his gaze to the man with NEUROLOGIST written on his white lab coat at the foot of the bed with Dr. Kearns, then to Liz who stood by the bedside holding Michael's hand. "I'm just tired. I don't need any tests. I want to go home."

Tears rolled down Liz's cheeks. She kissed Michael's hand and looked at Sin for guidance.

Sin let the door close. "Hey, bro. Why don't we let the doctors decide when you need to go home? Don't worry about the office. I called and told them one of us would check in with them later today."

"You included me?" Surprise widened Michael's eyes.

Sin placed his hand on his brother's bare shoulder where the hospital gown had slipped off. "You're still in charge."

Michael nodded and eased back on the pillow. "Like I said, things have been hectic, especially with so many of our clients going to the ESPY Awards this week."

Liz's startled gaze flew up to Sin's. The ESPYs were over.

Sin turned to the watchful doctors and introduced

himself. "Thank you, Dr. Kearns, for going over last night."

The dark-haired man in his early fifties nodded, but his frown didn't clear. "You made the right call. This is Dr. Crenshaw, a neurologist; I called him in to consult with me."

"Dr. Crenshaw."

"Mr. Sinclair." The handshake was firm. "I've ordered some blood work and other tests, but from what I understand there is a family history."

Sin's chest had that tight feeling again. "Why don't we discuss it someplace else?"

Michael reared up on the bed, his eyes wide. "Don't you dare tell them. I don't have it."

Sin came back to the bed. "I have to, Michael. They have to know so they can help you."

"I said no, goddammit."

"Michael," Liz began, but Michael cut her off.

"You get me out of here, Liz. You get me out of here now!" he yelled, looking wildly around the room.

Dr. Kearns rang the nurses' station. "Please bring Mr. Sinclair his sedation *stat*."

Michael was shaking his head. "I don't want that shit! You're trying to make me think I have it, and I don't!"

"Michael." Sin had never felt so lost or inept. He swallowed the huge lump in his throat. This was his big brother who had always been there for him. "You know we love you."

The hospital door opened and in came a nurse. In her hand was a hypodermic needle.

"No." Michael threw back the bedding and tried to get out of bed.

Fighting tears and misery, Sin restrained Michael with Dr. Crenshaw's help. "It's all right, Michael."

"No." Michael twisted away, but Dr. Kearns held his arm as the nurse uncapped the syringe.

"No, Payton. Please. Just take me home."

Sin blinked back tears as the needle slid into Michael's upper forearm. His brother's body jerked, his accusing gaze pinned on Sin.

"Why are you letting them do this to me? There's nothing wrong with me. I promise I won't die like my father, not knowing my own name, unable to take care of myself. I won't!" The last words were screamed as tears rolled down Michael's cheeks. "I don't have Huntington's. I don't."

Sin just held on to Michael and prayed for strength, because his prayer that Michael would be all right would not be answered.

Ten excruciatingly long minutes later, Sin walked out of Michael's room with his arm around an unsteady Liz. Michael's primary care doctor had turned his care over to Dr. Crenshaw. He was the one who could help Michael now, although there was pitifully little that could be done. Sin and Liz were to meet him in his office later. Neither he nor Liz had wanted to leave until they were sure Michael was asleep. The twins and Liz's parents converged on them as soon as the door opened.

"What's the matter with Dad?"

"We heard him shouting."

Sin wasn't sure if he or Liz jerked. Neither wanted the boys to know what was wrong with their father.

"We couldn't hear what he said," explained Liz's father, his face lined with worry. He wore a golf shirt, plaid pants, and golf shoes. Retired, he played at his club every day, weather permitting.

His wife preferred tennis at the club and had never worked a day in her life, just opened her arms to their only child. "It's going to be all right. The doctors will find out what's wrong with Michael and he'll be just fine."

Liz burrowed closer. "Oh, Mama."

"Can we see Dad now?" asked Jadon.

"You said we could see him later," Jardon reminded her.

Sin watched Michael's wife slowly lift her head and close her red eyes. She'd been spoiled and as sheltered as her mother. She'd married Michael after graduating from college. She'd never had to face life's harsh realities without her parents or Michael, or both.

"Liz, I'll take them in." Sin opened the door. Perhaps it was a good idea for them to see their father calm instead of the raving stranger he had been the night before. The twins followed him in. Their steps cautious, they stopped initially at the foot of the bed before going to stand on either side of their father.

"We're here, Dad. Mom wouldn't let us come in before."

"Don't worry. You'll be up in time for our first game. You promised and you've never broken a promise."

Sin couldn't take any more. Michael loved his kids. It was going to hurt him immeasurably when he realized the burden he had placed on them. "Let's let your father rest." Neither moved.

"You sure he's going to be all right?"

"He just doesn't look the same."

"It's the sedative." Sin opened the door. "You can see him later."

After one last look, the twins left the room and went straight for their mother. Sin was sure they hadn't hugged and clung to her like that in a long time. He remembered all too well himself and Michael doing the same thing when they left their father's room the day he'd been finally diagnosed.

"Mr. and Mrs. Kessler, would you mind taking the boys home with you?" Sin asked. "Liz and I have to talk to the doctor."

"We don't mind staying."

"Maybe he'll wake up and wonder where we are."

Liz tried to smile at her sons and failed miserably. "He'll be asleep for a while. You go with your grandparents. You have football practice later today." The twins started to protest; their mother cut them off. "You know how proud he is of you. He wouldn't want you to miss practice."

"I can take you, boys," their grandfather said. "I'd like to see you in action."

"Afterward we can go get something to eat at that restaurant you like," their grandmother added.

"I'll tell Michael where you are when he wakes up," Sin said. "Don't worry, I plan to stay with him."

"Off you go," Liz said. "Sin and I have to see the doctor."

"He's gonna make Dad better. Right?" asked Jadon.

"Yes," Liz answered after a moment. The lies had begun.

"We'll begin genetic testing later this afternoon along with other diagnostic studies," Dr. Crenshaw said, his hands folded as he gazed over his desk at Sin. "Have you been tested?"

"No," Sin clipped out. "I don't need to be. I can't have children. I have a living will. One of my best friends has power of attorney if I become ill."

"That's your decision. The uncertainty can be as stressful as the burdensome knowledge that you carry the hereditary gene." His attention shifted to Liz, her head down, hands clasped together as she sat next to Sin in front of the desk. "You have sixteen-year-old twins."

Her head jerked up. Her eyes were as wild as Michael's when she jerked around to Sin. "No. No."

Sin reached for his sister-in-law's hand, felt it tremble, her nails bite into the back of his hand. It would only get harder on all of them.

"Mrs. Sinclair, I'm sorry, but you have to face the possibility even though testing isn't usually recommended until eighteen years of age," the doctor said softly. "If your children didn't inherit the faulty gene, they can't develop the disease or pass it on to their children. If the test results show your husband has Huntington's, the chances of your children having the mutated gene are fifty–fifty."

Tears streamed down her cheeks. "Michael was so sure. So sure. We planned to grow old together. Spoil our grandchildren." She shook her head. "I can't do this to the boys right now. I can't."

"You don't have to." Sin's voice was tight. "We'll work this out some way to protect the twins until they're old enough to make their own decision." Sin looked at the doctor. "I don't want *any* information given out about Michael or his condition."

Obviously offended, Dr. Crenshaw leaned back in his executive chair. "We value and honor patient rights. You have my guarantee."

"If not, the lawyer I spoke of will be talking to your lawyers and it won't be pretty. You have *my* guarantee."

He isn't going to call.

Hands clasped in her lap, Summer sat behind her desk and stared at the crystal clock that her father had given to her mother on their first wedding anniversary. She hadn't even made it two weeks with Sin.

She swallowed. It was almost 4:00 PM. She hadn't left her office since she arrived and had no idea what she wanted to wear for the restaurant's opening at five. She reached for the phone on her desk, heard the dial tone, then replaced the receiver. Next, she stared at her cell phone and saw the smiling wedding picture of her parents. Looking at them had gotten her through her some rough times.

For the thousandth time she wished her parents were there. She could talk to her mother about her turbulent feelings. Talk her father out of finding Sin and beating him to a pulp for making her cry.

"I miss you." Her thumb grazed across the screen, then she placed the phone back on her desk. "Quitting wasn't in either of your vocabularies. You went after what you wanted. I have to be just as strong and determined."

A call to Alex earlier that morning hadn't revealed any more information. She'd used the excuse of hiring another chef and wanted him to handle the non-disclosure contract as usual. He'd asked about Sin, proving he didn't know that Sin had left town. Whatever it was, he was dealing with it alone. She hurt for him, but until he contacted her or she found out where he was, she was helpless.

She rose to her feet. She wasn't giving up on Sin calling. He'd looked like he was living his worst nightmare when he turned to her that morning. His leaving hadn't been some whim. His family needed him.

So did she.

Sin watched Michael sleep in the suite he'd had him moved to, hoping the bigger and more luxurious surroundings would help calm him. At least for a little while they had.

When Michael had awakened, he'd been confused and scared instead of angry. Thankfully, he'd agreed to sign the consent for the battery of tests Dr. Crenshaw had ordered. Unlike Sin, Michael hadn't designated anyone to have power of attorney for him. He'd even joked that Sin was going to owe him big. But behind the laughter was the fear.

Sin had fully understood when, after picking at his lunch, Michael went back to sleep. All of them were hoping against hope that something else had triggered the outburst, the lapses of memory. Liz held on to that hope and felt hopeful enough to leave Michael for a bit and go downstairs to the cafeteria. Sin was content with the coffee. Food was the farthest thing from his mind.

After checking on a sleeping Michael, Sin sat on the short leather sofa and pulled out his phone. There were several messages. The ones that made his heart clench, his arms ache with loneliness were from Summer.

Please call me.

No recriminations, no intrusive questions, just there if he needed her. He did. Badly.

Closing his eyes, he leaned his head back on the sofa, and for one weak moment wished her there, his head on her shoulder, her arms around him.

Then what?

Shaking his head, he accepted that Summer was out of his life for good. He couldn't tell her the truth. She'd worry, then push her way into his life no matter what he wanted. She valued and loved her friends. She'd want to be there if anyone needed her.

He blew out a resigned breath. He should have been stronger, but even as the thought ran through his mind, he knew he'd always cherish the time they had spent together.

And wish they had one more night, another morning to hear her laughter, see the smile on her face that brightened up his day.

He glanced at his brother, who was still sleeping. Time had run out for both of them.

Later that afternoon Sin checked in with his New York office, and then the Dallas office Michael ran. Sin gave Michael's assistant, Steve Brody, the speech he'd rehearsed. "Michael isn't feeling well. He'll be out of the office for a few days so call me if there's a problem you need his help on. I'm in town and will be available twenty-four seven."

"Don't worry, Payton, we'll take care of things

on this end," Steve assured him. "Tell Michael we got his back. I'm glad he decided to take it easy."

There was something in Steve's voice. "Why is that?"

"Er, no particular reason."

He was lying. Sin had played enough cards with Steve to know he couldn't bluff worth a damn, but he had excellent managerial skills and knew player stats as well as he knew the birthdays of his five children, whose pictures cluttered his desk. "What happened at work, Steve? I need the truth the first time. I don't want to drag it out of you."

"Michael is a great guy who's on top of things and keeps us all in line and on task," Steve quickly said.

"Steve, what did I say about not dragging it out of you?"

There was a pause, then, "All right. He's been a little irritable lately, forgotten a couple of appointments. Nothing that couldn't be rescheduled," Steve rushed on to say. "Like he said, he just needed a little break. I'm glad he's getting it."

"Yeah. I'll tell him what you said, and Steve."

He hesitated. Sin wasn't known for his patience. "Yes, Payton."

"I'm glad you're loyal to Michael and think so highly of him. It means a lot to both of us. He is a great guy. Bye." Sin disconnected the call. He had one more to make.

He purposefully saved it for the last. He walked

to a window that showed the corner of a park and the front of another building in the huge hospital complex, which was touted to be the one of the best in the nation. Aware he was putting off the call, he quickly pushed in the number.

"Hey, Sin," Alex answered. "I'm needed back into court in five so make it quick."

Sin tried, but the words refused to form in his brain.

"Sin?"

He heard the question in Alex's voice. He'd told him about his suspicions about Michael. "Mike is in the hospital."

Alex cursed. "I suppose you're there."

"Yes."

"What hospital? I should be out of here by five. I'll book the first flight heading to Dallas."

"No." Sin glanced at Michael to ensure he was sleeping, then stared back out the window. "I can handle this."

"Bull," Alex rasped. Sin heard what he thought were the hinges of a door opening or closing. "Stop being so effing noble."

"Easy, counselor." Alex seldom lost his cool or cursed. With his killer stare and keen intelligence, he didn't have to do either to get his point across.

"Hell, you're my friend, and the world just dropped on your head."

Sin worked the tight muscles in his shoulders. "I always suspected this was coming."

"My point exactly. You've lived with this burden for years while Michael and his family went on their merry way. You're sacrificed your happiness for them. Made sure they were taken care of, even seeing that they didn't have to care for you if you became ill." There was a brief pause. "Summer, oh my goodness, Summer. Tell me you weren't that big of a fool not to tell her?"

"You know I couldn't." Sin stared out at the lights in another building in the hospital complex as they came on.

"People who care about each other don't stop because of problems," Alex told him.

"Let it go, Alex. I just wanted you to know. You might have to exert that power of attorney sooner rather than later."

The silence was deafening. "Are you having symptoms?"

"No, my thoughts are crystal clear, my hands steady, my memory intact." *So much better to feel the big hole where my heart used to be.*

"Sin, Michael has his wife and children, his wife has the children and her parents, the twins have their mother and grandparents. Who do you have?"

Sin's head pressed against the cool glass. "Like I said, I've always known it would be this way."

"Hurting people who love you? Shutting them out of your life?"

He was too tired to take offense. "I don't expect you to understand."

"Damn right. What hospital?"

This was his alone. His duty.

Since Sin was younger, if Michael did have the defective gene, he'd become ill first. His mother, with tears in her eyes on her deathbed, had begged Sin to look after his brother. To do what she couldn't do for their father. He would have in any case, but he would have promised anything to ease the guilt in her eyes. She, like the doctors, thought his father was mentally ill.

"Tell me what hospital."

Sin straightened. "The nurse is coming. Goodbye."

Sin disconnected the call, shutting off Alex's yelling for him not to hang up the damn phone. Lord, he hurt. He turned to look at Michael. How could they get through this and remain a close-knit family?

A little voice told him they wouldn't.

Alex cursed, seriously considered kicking the bathroom wall. He was angry at Sin. Angry at the impossible position he was in. Huntington's could happen early in life, but it was more likely to occur from age thirty to middle age. Because Sin's father had the hereditary disease, Sin had refused to have more than a passing relationship with a woman.

He'd denied himself because if his brother had the defective gene, then Sin knew his sister-in-law wouldn't be able to cope emotionally or financially.

If the unlucky lot fell to Sin, he hadn't wanted to burden a woman or his brother and his family. He'd assigned Alex power of attorney. Signed a living will.

In every equation Sin had put himself last. "Sin, I could kick your—"

Alex cursed again and pressed in a phone number he knew well. Sin would go to the mat for them, but he wasn't giving his friends the same opportunity. He'd soon find out what true friendship meant.

"Man Hunters. Luke Grayson."

"Luke. Alex. I need you to find someone."

Chapter 14

Sin, feet propped up on the small table in front of the sofa, watched the sports channel with Michael. The Texas Rangers were playing the Red Sox. With the commentator's play-by-play account, not talking to each other wasn't so oppressive. A couple of times Michael had commented on a particularly idiotic comment from one announcer or the other.

Sin wanted to pump his fist on those occasions. Michael was still there. Sin clung to those moments. Progression of the disease varied.

A light knock sounded on the door. Sin expected the door to open and to see a nurse coming to check Michael's vital signs or give him medication. He hoped it wasn't more blood work. Perhaps because the gene was detected through the blood, Michael always became agitated when he saw the lab tech.

Michael muttered his displeasure. "It's almost ten."

"You're just a popular guy." Sin's feet hit the floor and he stretched his hands over his head. "Come in."

The door swung open and Alex stood there, his hand on the door. "I see I have the right room."

Surprise had Sin dropping his arms as if they held fifty-pound weights.

"Can I come in?" Alex asked.

"You alone?" Sin inquired, trying to look behind Alex's frame.

"Aren't I enough?" Alex asked, letting the door swing shut. "Hey, Michael. Thought you could use some of those candied pecans you like so much."

Michael took the handled bag, his questioning gaze going back to Sin. "You knew I was here?"

"Sorry to intrude." Alex lifted his briefcase. "I have papers for Sin to sign that couldn't wait. The screwup Glen Atkins fired Sin last night and I need to send Sin's acceptance, but I need a signature."

"You called it right," Michael said slowly as if the words were difficult to form. "Atkins was on the news."

Alex pulled up a chair by Michael's bed. 'You should have seen Sin in action. Your little brother laid the loudmouth flat in two seconds with his karate moves."

"We used to love those kung fu movies with Bruce Lee," Michael said slowly.

"Me, too, but I'd never have the coordination to pull off those maneuvers." Alex pointed to the television screen. "Looks like a good game. I guess I can root for the Rangers since they're not playing our Yankees." Alex stood. "I'll let you watch in peace and get that signature."

"We can sit over here." Sin motioned to the small sofa across the room. He waited until Alex sat next to him, until he was sure Michael's attention was on the game. "You could have sent them in an attachment for me to sign and return or overnighted them."

Alex handed him a pen and the letter. "I wasn't sure you were checking e-mail."

Taking the pen, Sin drew the papers toward him. "How did you find Michael?"

"Man Hunters."

Sin signed the release and handed it and the pen back to Alex. "I forgot about your sister's husband. So you caught a flight and here you are."

Alex's lips quirked. "My sister's sister-in-law is married to Blade Navarone, who happened to have a business acquaintance with a jet and pilot in New York to put at my disposal. The pilot is at the Ritz, getting some rest. We leave at six in the morning."

"You didn't—"

"I didn't. I simply said I needed a jet to Dallas. No other explanation was needed." Alex put the papers away. "Have you called Summer yet?"

Sin rose and went to the window. Alex was on his heels. "I told you that's over."

"So why were you so disappointed when you saw I was alone?"

"I thought C. J. might be with you."

"Liar, and don't you dare pull that kung fu move on me. Dianne insisted on coming on this 'unexpected business trip' and she won't be pleased to see me bruised and battered."

Sin shoved his hand over his head. "So, it will take a while for me to get over her."

"How about forever?"

Sin turned and went to take a seat by his brother's bed. "Who's winning?"

"Score is tied." Michael looked at Sin. "I want to go home."

Sin came to his feet. "I know, man. Soon. I promise."

"Yeah." Michael pulled the covers up over his shoulder and turned away.

Sin felt the hand on his shoulder. At least for a little while, he wouldn't be alone.

"It's after one, I better leave so you can get some sleep." Alex rose to his feet.

Sin stood and stuck out his hand. "Thanks."

Alex glanced at the hand, then pulled Sin to him in a one-armed hug. "If I didn't have court tomorrow, I wouldn't leave."

"I know." Sin stepped back. "You better get to Dianne. I admire her restraint. She hasn't called once."

"She trusts and loves me, and knows I feel the same way," Alex told him. "Nothing can compare to having someone that's connected to you."

Sin's mouth tightened. "Give it a rest, Alex. I'll walk you to the door."

"She deserves to know."

"No." Sin's features hardened. "No, and you better not tell her or I'll sue your butt off."

"That's twice tonight you've questioned my integrity." Alex's free hand caught Sin's arm. "You cannot do this by yourself. You're hurting, on edge, and who the hell could blame you. Having friends will help. Don't shut us out."

"It's the only way I know how to get through this." He stepped back, breaking the hold. "Just tell everyone I had to leave town unexpectedly."

"That won't satisfy any of the people who care about you." Alex's fingers tightened on the briefcase. "And Summer deserves more."

"Drop it, Alex, or we're going to find out about Dianne's reaction to you being bruised and battered."

"Once she learned it was you, she'd be down here and in your face for harming a hair on my head," Alex came back.

Sin almost smiled. "You're a good friend, but please let me do this the only way I can at the moment."

Alex's sigh was long and deep. "All right. If you need me to do anything, you better call or I'm going to be pissed at you."

Sin did smile. "You've used more un-Alex-like language today than in our entire friendship. Now, get out of here so Dianne won't worry."

"Remember to call, and you had better pick up if I call you."

"Safe travel."

"I love you, man, and you better not forget." With a brisk nod, Alex opened the door. It slowly swung shut.

Alex swiped his key card in the door of his hotel room and pushed it open. He'd barely turned from shutting the door before Dianne was there, her arms wrapped tightly around him.

'I love you, Alex."

The briefcase fell from his hands and he held his wife in his arm. When he told her he had to travel to Dallas to see a client, she'd taken one look at his face and asked if he minded if she came. He'd told her to pack an overnight bag.

He already knew what Sin had yet to accept: Having someone close when life kicked you in the teeth helped you get through those bad times. "I'm sorry I didn't call."

"When my life fell apart, you were there to patiently support me until I was strong enough to stand on my own." She kissed the smooth line of his jaw. "I didn't realize until later how much courage that took, how much faith you had in me."

"I could not fail to be there for you. I love you," he told her.

"You a fantastic lawyer and friend because you care about the person. Don't ever forget it."

Lifting his head, he stared down into the eyes of the woman he would love through eternity. "Loving you is the easiest and best thing I've ever done."

"I never knew what real happiness was until I knew you'd be mine forever—that no matter what, you'd be there."

Her words played in his head. *No matter what, you'd be there.* Alex thought of Sin alone in the hospital. He needed his friends, but more than that he needed the woman he couldn't forget. If Sin didn't come to his senses, Alex would find a way to bring them together without breaking client confidentiality.

Summer had a restless night, and her morning wasn't much better. She'd slept in Sin's T-shirt and fought tears and misery most of the night. When her alarm went off she was more than ready to dress and go to work. She needed to think of something besides the possibility of Sin not coming back.

Once she arrived at the restaurant, she went straight for the kitchen to bake the specialty cakes instead of waiting. She didn't want to listen to her own thoughts.

She'd heard enough to realize it was a family

emergency, but she didn't understand why he'd shut her out. In times of problems, families draw closer. She'd called his office and left numerous messages—which were never returned. Had she been so needy that she had seen more in Sin's eyes, felt more in his touch, than there had been?

Baking always calmed her, took her mind off whatever was bothering her. An hour later she had three inedible, very flat cake layers. She'd left out the baking powder.

"Are you all right, Summer?" Daphne asked.

Blinking rapidly to keep from crying, Summer glanced up at her manager, who apparently was the only one brave enough to ask. The women in the kitchen wore sympathetic expressions, the men angry ones. It wasn't hard to figure out what was bothering her. The restaurant had been buzzing—in an excited way—about her and Sin.

Picking up the ruined cakes, she went to the garbage and scraped each into the trash. "Just having an off day."

Daphne took the pan from Summer. "I'll do this."

"I'll fix you a cup of tea," Joan said.

"You go to your office, I'll bring it," Karen said.

"For lunch, I'll prepare your favorite salad," Kerri added.

Summer glanced around the kitchen. She thought they might look away, but no one did. Just as on the night she had driven the van to the shelter, they were concerned. They were more than employees, they were friends.

"Thank you." She took the pan from Daphne. "We have a restaurant to run. I'd appreciate the tea after I finish these cakes. Radcliffe's customers expect the best, and we'll give it to them."

"You have an appointment in thirty minutes to meet with Cicely and Dianne at the bridal gown shop," Daphne reminded her and took the pan back. "I'll clean up the pans. Do you want to make a fresh batch?"

She could have left something else out. The reputation of Radcliffe's was too important to take a chance. She pulled off her apron. "Please pour out the batter. I'll be back as soon as I can to mix a fresh batch."

Summer headed for her office to touch up her makeup and grab her purse, hoping her misery didn't show in her face. *Please, don't let me ruin this for Cicely.*

Summer waved to Cicely and Dianne standing on the sidewalk in front of the bridal salon. "Sorry I'm late."

"We both just arrived." Cicely faced the show window. "We were looking at this one until you and C. J.'s mother arrived, but it's not me."

"You're not the ruffle type," Dianne said. "What do you think, Summer?"

Summer turned to look at the off-the-shoulder

wedding gown with tiers of tulle on the skirt. The dress wasn't Cicely, but she'd find the perfect one. Summer would never have that opportunity, never have that magical moment when she walked down the aisle to Sin and he was unable to take his eyes off her. Tears clouded her vision.

She swallowed. Swallowed again, but the tears still crested in her eyes.

"Summer." Cicely's arm went around her shoulder.

Pulling a tissue from her handbag, Summer wiped away the tears. "I'm sorry. I'm a terrible maid of honor."

"Nonsense," Cicely said. "I cried tears over C. J."

"All relationships hit rough patches." Dianna took the tissue from Summer's hand and wiped away fresh tears.

"It's—it's more than a rough spot." Briefly she shut her eyes, then looked at Cicely. "He says it's over. That's why I came over the other morning."

"We suspected something had happened, but C. J. is going to stay out of it." Cicely leaned her head against Summer's. "He remembers I broke up with him because I was scared of trusting my feelings, of trusting our love."

"If anyone says falling in love and trusting another person with your heart isn't scary, they're lying or don't know what true love is." Dianna dabbed another tear from Summer's cheek. "Give him time."

"He won't accept my calls." Summer sniffed.

"I-I think he needs me, and that hurts most of all. He's shutting me out."

"You might be right," Dianne mused.

Alerted by Dianne's strained tone and her furrowed brow, Summer took Dianne's shoulders. "You know something?"

"I can't explain, and please don't ask me to." Dianne bit her lower lip.

"Alex." Summer let her hands fall. Her mind raced. She remembered snippets of the conversation. Had Sin needed a recommendation for a lawyer for his brother? Sin was in trouble and all she could do was wait and hope he'd contact her—which didn't seem likely to happen. She pressed her hand against Dianne's. "I won't. I'd appreciate it if you'd let me know if you find out that Sin is back in New York."

"You got it."

Summer nodded. "Thank you. At least I know he's not alone."

A black Lincoln pulled up to the curb. The driver quickly rounded the car and opened the back door. Out stepped C. J.'s mother. She was fashionable as always in a beige-and-gold tweed Chanel suit. She hugged the waiting women. "Sorry I'm late. Traffic." She took Cicely's hands. "You ready?"

Cicely nodded. "I've been ready all my life. I'm just finding it out."

C. J.'s mother reached for the gold latch of her designer bag. Summer gave her a tissue. Mrs. Callahan lightly dabbed her eyes. "Thank you, Summer. I promised myself I wouldn't do this." She frowned, then palmed Summer's cheeks. "I see you've shed a few tears as well. One day we'll be looking for your wedding gown."

Summer somehow managed to smile, felt Dianne catch her hand, and Cicely briefly touch her arm. "In the meantime, let's go find the perfect gown for Cicely." Summer opened the heavy glass door for her aunt and her friends, then followed them inside the boutique.

The odds of her looking for a wedding gown in the near or distant future were slim to none. The man she loved wanted nothing to do with her.

Chapter 15

The next morning, Sin followed the gurney carrying Michael into the hall. Michael was silent, the fear obvious in his eyes. The same fear Sin saw in Liz's nervous gestures, her fingering of the diamond necklace Michael had given her.

"Michael is going to be all right. He has to be." Liz turned to Sin outside Michael's hospital door. "Maybe it's a tumor, like the boys think."

"Liz—"

"No." She held up her hand to stop him. "That's the only thing that's keeping me going. I'm not sure I can handle it if it's what you think."

"Liz, Michael needs you now. More than ever." Sin placed his hand on her tense shoulder.

Anger flared in her dark eyes. "He shouldn't have put me and the twins in this awful position."

She was right, but that didn't change one thing. "Have you decided what you're going to tell people?"

She glanced away. "I'm certainly not going to tell them what you think. I'm not scaring the boys or having our friends whispering about us. We'll say the doctor is still running tests—which he is."

"If they come back conclusive?"

"They won't." Brushing by him, she hurried to catch up with the gurney. Sin followed.

Michael had a battery of tests scheduled that day and the next. Sin and Liz went with him for each one. Waiting, Sin caught up on his phone calls, checked in with his offices. Business was thriving. Companies and athletes' agents hadn't stopped calling.

His phone rang. He saw C. J.'s name and hesitated, then found a quiet corner and connected the call. "Hey."

"Hey, yourself. Where are you?"

"Dallas," he slowly answered, already knowing what was coming next. "I'm thinking about making this my main office for a few months."

"Any particular reason for the sudden change?" C. J. asked.

Sin had to give him points for not threatening to pull out his tonsils though his nose. He'd thought long and hard about his answer. "I've just spread myself too thin lately. The Dallas office is the busiest, so it makes sense that I focus more here for the time being."

"What about Summer?"

Even knowing it was coming, the question almost took him to his knees. "I told her from the beginning that it wasn't forever."

"I wish you were standing in front of me."

"So you could bloody my nose?"

"Nope. To read you better. You aren't the impulsive type, so I'm going to ask you again, why the sudden need to stay in Dallas and hurt Summer in the process?"

"I've given you the only answer I can."

"That's BS. Maybe not today, but soon I'll be in your face and I'm going to get the truth. Later."

"Later." Sin ended the call and glanced down the hall where Michael was having an MRI. Running from the truth certainly hadn't helped his brother. It had only made things worse. Sin was doing the same thing. In asking Alex to keep Sin's secret, he'd placed his best friend in an impossible situation. It was time he took care of his affairs. He activated the phone.

"I need to leave for New York as early as possible tomorrow morning. Ready the jet."

Sin's jet touched down shortly after seven the next morning. He hurried down the steps and quickly got into the waiting car that merged into the slow-moving traffic into Manhattan.

He'd already called Alex and asked him to bring C. J. to Sin's office. As soon as he spoke with them, and went by his place to pick up a few things, he was flying back to Dallas. The hour time difference was in his favor coming and going. He didn't want to be away from Michael or Liz too long. Both were holding on by a thread.

The car pulled to the curb in front of his office building. Sin was on the sidewalk before the driver got out. C. J. and Alex were waiting on him. "Thank you for coming. We'll talk in my office."

On the elevator, Sin felt the tension and stared straight ahead. In his office, he went behind his desk and placed his briefcase on top. He looked at his two best friends, the men who meant so much to him, and couldn't get the words out.

"What's going on, Sin?" C. J. asked, his hands on his waist, a worried frown on his face. "You look like hell and Alex isn't looking much better."

"Give him a moment," Alex said, a flicker of pain in his eyes.

C. J.'s eyes narrowed, stepped closer to the desk. "You in trouble?"

"Something like that." Sin came from around the desk. "Have you ever heard of Huntington's disease?" At C. J.'s puzzled expression, Sin explained the inherited progressive, degenerative disease. He ended by saying, "My father was diagnosed when I was eighteen. Neither Michael nor I was tested. He's showing symptoms. That's why I'm relocating for a few months."

"Summer." C. J. caught Sin's jacket lapels. "How could you do that to her?"

"C. J.—"

"Shut it, Alex," C. J. snarled. "Knowing you could get sick and you still touched her?"

"Yes. Because I talked myself into believing that maybe it would be all right, that Michael's symptoms were stress-related, that Summer and I were both adult enough to handle my leaving one day. She was the one thing in life that I couldn't walk away from—until Michael called me the other morning, angry and hysterical."

"Could you have walked away from Cicely?" Alex asked quietly.

"Damn." C. J. released Sin's lapels, then paced away, then back, shoved his hands over his head. "You feel all right, though, right?"

"For the moment," Sin said.

C. J. grabbed him again. "Don't you dare get sick. I mean it! I'll kick your butt."

"If I do, Alex has power of attorney. I didn't want to burden anyone," Sin said, trying for levity. "Since he's also my lawyer, he got the short straw."

"Because I'm your friend, I'll ignore that insult." Alex walked to him.

"Sin—" C. J. scrubbed his hand over his face. "You know I speak before I think sometimes. Summer really cares about you. You should tell her."

"No." Sin shook his head. "I've known for a long time that no woman would want to share my life. It wouldn't be fair to her. I'm flying back shortly. I'd appreciate it if you didn't tell Summer that I was here until I'm gone. When I can, I'll write her a letter and explain."

"A letter," C. J. said incredulously.

"Believe me, it's for the best all around if I don't see her." He stuck out his hand. "Thanks for coming."

C. J. ignored the hand and hugged Sin. "You take care of yourself. You call."

"I will." Sin straightened.

Alex gave him a hug. "We're here for you, Sin. If you need us, don't think, just call."

He nodded. For him, this was good-bye. He'd always known he'd have to go through this alone. He walked them to the door. "Alex, keep C. J. out of trouble."

"You're my best man, that's your job," C. J. said, his eyes probing. "You go take care of your brother and then you come back. You're giving me a blow-out bachelor party, remember?"

Sin tried to smile. There was no telling what his life would be like next year. "I remember."

"Let's get out of here." Alex caught Sin's eye, dipped his head, and moved through the door with a reluctant C. J. "We'll be praying for you, Sin."

"Thanks." Sin closed the door, then went to his desk, each step an effort. He checked his watch. His secretary should be there shortly. He'd already spoken with his office manager, who would take over for the time being. He had good people. The office would be fine without him. After he went by his place to pick up the mementos of Summer he'd hoarded, he was leaving. They were all he'd ever have of her.

The knock on the door surprised him, then he realized it was probably his office manager. "Come in."

The door opened and Summer walked in, more beautiful than he remembered. His breath caught. His body wanted, needed. He started around his desk before he caught himself and abruptly stopped. She wasn't for him. "I don't think we had an appointment."

"You didn't return my phone calls."

"Because playtime is over." He saw her wince, and fought to remain cold and impersonal. This was for her. "I'm sorry if you expected more. I told you from the beginning, this wasn't forever."

"It wasn't even two weeks."

And the memories would have to last him a lifetime. "If you'll excuse me, I need to get quite a few things done before I fly back to Dallas."

"Is—is your brother all right?"

His head snapped up. If she had talked to C. J. or Alex, she would know the answer to that question. "How did you know I was here?"

"Cicely and Dianne both called and said you were meeting with Alex and C. J. I came over so we could talk."

Sin realized too late that he hadn't asked Alex and C. J. not to tell their wives. "There's nothing to talk about. I really am busy. Good-bye."

* * *

Summer stared at Sin, his gaze fixed over her shoulder. She realized he hadn't looked at her directly since she'd walked into his office. There had to be a reason. She went to him, touched his face, felt the shiver of his body, saw the flash of desire in his eyes he was unable to hide. He wasn't as disinterested as he wanted her to believe.

"I love you," she simply said.

If she hadn't been watching his face she might not have seen the brief flare of happiness before it was replaced by sorrow. He went behind his desk and began shoving papers into a briefcase. "We were just having fun. I'm turning this office over to someone else." He snapped the case shut. "I won't be back."

"Is your brother that sick?"

He flinched. She thought she saw fear in his eyes. "You called his name when you were talking to him on the phone. Later you said, *Call an ambulance for him*," she explained.

"Stay out of what doesn't concern you."

"Why won't you tell me what's going on?"

"Let it go!"

"I can't. I won't. What changed between the time I went to sleep in your arms and your brother's phone call?"

His eyes snapped with fury. The impossible situation finally pushed him over the edge. "You want to know so badly, I'll tell you. Michael might have

Huntington's Disease, the same hereditary disease that killed our father at fifty-nine. His wife is scared she's losing her husband, scared for their twins who might also carry the defective gene."

"What—what about you?" She could barely form the words, speak them. Fear clutched at her.

"There's a fifty–fifty chance I carry the defective gene as well. I haven't had the test and I'm not going to. Find someone else to love."

She dashed away the tears in her eyes. She ached for him, his family. "You have my love whether you want it or not. You can't live your life being afraid. You take and give joy and love as long as you can. If it happens, at least you have someone you love by your side. You love in spite of, not because of."

"Well, count yourself lucky."

"Lucky!" she snapped. "Lucky that you're walking out on me without giving us a chance? My parents died before they were forty. They left the house to go to a movie and never returned."

"Summer, don't." His face contorted with remorse. He reached for her.

She batted his hands away. "Don't you dare touch me. I'm mad at you. Mad that you don't have enough faith in me to know that I'd be there no matter what."

"That's just it. I do. I can't burden you with this."

"If our places were reversed, how would you feel if I shut you out?"

He flinched. "That's supposition. This is real. My sister-in-law is barely holding on."

"And you're trying to take care of all of them, just as you took care of me. I understand and admire that about you, but you don't have to go through it alone." She shoved her hand through her hair. "Your sister-in-law loves your brother, but she's also had good years with him, had their children. When you take that plane back to Dallas, what are you leaving me with besides heartache?"

"I can't have children." He watched shock race over her face. "I had a vasectomy as soon as I was twenty-one." He wanted to turn away. "I wasn't going to take a chance and pass it on to a child."

"You said you haven't been tested."

His mouth tightened into a narrow line. "I haven't. I won't. That's one area Michael and I agree on. I don't want to know."

"But he had his family while you've denied yourself really caring for a woman."

"Until you. I'm sorry."

"For making love with me or for leaving me?" she asked tightly.

"Both."

"You know what I'm sorry for? I'm sorry that the man I fell in love with, the man I'll love forever, doesn't know or trust me well enough to understand that he's condemning me to never being truly happy because he won't be there."

"Summer." He reached for her again.

"Don't Summer me. You taught me to fight. Well, dammit, I want you to fight for us. Give us this time. If . . . if it turns out . . ." She squeezed her eyes shut for a brief second. "Don't make us live without each other. Give us a chance and, if the worst happens, we go through it together the best we can."

"I can't."

She took a deep breath. "Answer me one question truthfully and I'll leave."

"Sum—"

"You owe me that."

"All right."

"Do you love me?"

Sin flinched. His body stiffened.

"I deserve the truth."

He walked behind his desk. "Yes."

She swallowed. "Then don't make me go through life with only my memories of the time we spent together. Believe in me, in us."

He wanted to so badly. She deserved the happiness he couldn't give her. "It's over."

Her shoulders sagged. Her head lowered, then lifted. "I'm not giving up on us. I love you even more now because I know the reason for the shadows in your eyes. When you realize we're better together than apart, I'll be waiting." She started for the door, heard his phone ring, once, twice. As she reached the door, it rang a third time.

"Aren't you going to answer that?" She didn't wait for his response. "I'm not going anyplace until you do."

Sin jerked the phone from inside his coat. The readout sent chills though him. "Payton Sinclair."

"Mr. Sinclair, it's Dr. Crenshaw."

"Yes. Is Michael all right? Did he have another episode?"

"I'm calling because the test results came back a little while ago. I'm sorry to say they came back positive. Your brother has Huntington's. I just informed him and his wife. I think it would be a wise decision for you to return to the hospital."

Anger rushed though Sin. "Why didn't you wait to tell him the test results until I was there?"

"Your brother insisted,"

"Because he was hoping I was wrong." Sin rubbed his hand over his face. "You should have waited."

"I'm sorry. It's rare that the results come back this quickly since it's done by an outside lab," Dr. Crenshaw said.

Another thought struck. "The twins. Their sons. Were they there?"

"No, that was another reason they wanted to know right away—the boys were with their grandparents. I gave your brother a sedative and ordered a milder one for his wife. I'm going back in there once I finish talking with you. I've called Dr. Kearns, and the hospital chaplain."

He should have been there. "I'm in New York. I'll get there as soon as I can."

"I'm sorry."

Sin hung up the phone, his chest tight, his gut

churning. He didn't realize for a moment that Summer had her arms around him. His eyes stung.

"I'm here, Sin. I'm here."

His arms went around her, clutching her to him. "I knew this was coming. Thought I could handle it."

Warm lips brushed against his. He felt cold. Adrift. "Reality is much harder to deal with than suspicion. Liz." He pulled away, hit speed dial. Paced until sister-in-law answered. Her sobs were heart wrenching. "Dr. Crenshaw just called me. I'm on my way. I'll call your parents and tell them to keep the boys away from the hospital until they hear from you. How's Michael?"

"The—the sedative is finally taking effect. Please hurry back."

"I'm leaving now." He hung up the phone to see Summer getting off hers.

"Let's go." She reached for his arm.

Instead of reaching for her as he wanted, he stepped back. "No."

She swiped at tears. "The first few days will be the hardest. I know that from losing my parents. You're angry, scared just like I was."

"I won't ruin your life."

"The only way you'll do that is by turning your back on our love." She went to him. "Whether on your jet or commercial, I'm going to Dallas. I've met Liz; I'd like to be there for her."

"What about your restaurant?"

"You need me. Nothing is more important than that." She took his arm and started for the door. "Let's go. I suppose the limo downstairs is waiting for you."

"Summer, I'm too tired to fight."

"Then don't. Let's put the lovers on hold and go see about your family. They need you."

He wanted her with him and he was too exhausted to keep battling with his conscience. "Let's go."

"You'll need a change of clothes."

Those were the only words Sin said to Summer on the way to her apartment. Once there, he'd gotten out first and just stood there clenching the door handle. He looked miserable and torn.

She slowly followed. "Please don't leave me."

"I'm not sure I could." Closing the car door, he took her arm and they went up to her apartment.

"It won't take me long." Hurrying to her bedroom, she grabbed a pair of black flats, black slacks, tops, undergarments and quickly put them in a bag, trying to listen for the door. Zipping up the case, she hurried back to the front room. She breathed a sigh of relief on seeing he was still there.

In minutes they were back in the car and pulling away. Sin stared out the window as if he had forgotten she was there. Then she remembered losing her parents and not wanting to talk at the time, recalled what he'd said in her apartment about leaving her.

I'm not sure I could. She slipped her hand under his, felt his tighten.

He wasn't shutting her out. For now, that was enough.

The flight to Dallas seemed endless. Sin would have been a raving maniac if not for Summer being with him. There were so many things going on in his head he couldn't form a coherent thought. She hadn't tried to talk or badger him into eating, she'd just sat beside him, offering her comfort and support. Yet he knew the hardest task lay ahead.

A little over four and a half hours after he'd spoken with Dr. Crenshaw, he stood outside his brother's hospital door. Sin wanted to see him, but hadn't the slightest notion what to say.

He felt Summer squeeze his hand and looked down into her face. She blinked back tears. "The words will come. Say what's in your heart. If Liz wants to go down for a cup of coffee or take a walk, I'm here."

Until that moment he hadn't realized how much he needed someone he didn't have to be strong in front of all the time, who understood what he was going through. "Thank you." Pushing open the door, he saw Michael with his arm over his eyes, Liz huddled in a chair five feet away from the bed. Yesterday, they'd always held hands.

"Hey, Michael. Liz."

Liz's head snapped up. She blinked, turned her head away. Michael flexed his fingers, but didn't move his arm. Both were hurting, but instead of drawing on each other as they'd done in the past, they were shutting each other out.

Just as Sin had done with Summer and his friends.

Letting the door close, Sin squeezed Liz's shoulder on the way to Michael's bed. For a moment, Sin felt helpless, overwhelmed; then he remembered the woman waiting outside.

You love in spite of, not because of.

"I love you, Michael. I've turned the New York office over to Jenson so I can be here with you. Together we'll figure out how to get through this."

Sin's heart squeezed when he saw tears seep from beneath Michael's arm. "Liz, you remember Summer Radcliffe, don't you? She owns Radcliffe's. I took you and Michael to her restaurant for your anniversary last year." They'd been so happy, so in love and excited to take their first vacation in years without the boys. Sin wanted her to remember those days and draw on them to give her the courage to go through this with Michael.

He glanced over his shoulder when she didn't respond. "At dinner, Michael gave you the necklace you're wearing." She seldom took it off.

Her fingers lightly touched the diamonds encircling her throat, then she lowered her hand. "Yes."

"She flew back with me. She's outside. Why don't you take a break?"

Without a word, Liz left the room without saying good-bye.

Seeing the ravaged face of Liz Sinclair, Summer's heart went out to her. She was a small, delicate woman. She looked angry, but beneath the anger was the fear. "Hello, Liz," Summer greeted. "We can walk, talk, or whatever. I realize we only met once, but I want to be here for you, if you'd like."

Liz arms were wrapped tightly around herself. "Are you and Payton involved?"

Summer hesitated for a moment, unsure of how Liz would react to the truth. "We were. Now, understandably, his focus is on Michael, you, and the twins."

Her eyes fired. "Take my advice and run like hell back to New York."

This wasn't a conversation Summer wanted to have in the hallway of a hospital. "Why don't we take a walk and we can talk."

"I'm scared, Sin. Not . . . not just about this." Michael's Adam's apple moved up and down as he swallowed, then swallowed again. "Liz. She's mad at me. She won't even talk to me since the doctor told us. I promised her I'd be all right, that our children would be all right." His arm lowered, tears and regret swam in his eyes. "The boys, Payton. I should have listened to you."

Sin gave the only truth he could. "We don't know

that the boys aren't all right. You love Liz and your children. You didn't know."

"And I was so cocky and sure." Michael dragged his arm across his eyes. "She'll come around, won't she, Payton?"

"She loves you," Sin said. "She has a lot to deal with. She's thinking about you and the boys."

Michael used the hem of the sheet to wipe his face. "Now I know why you never got serious."

"That changed a few weeks ago," Sin said and watched his brother's face as the information sank in. "Summer Radcliffe breaks all the rules for me. She knows about our family history and is sticking anyway. She was mad at me when I wanted to break it off. She loves me." Just saying the words, hearing them spoken out loud, helped.

"I'm happy for you. You deserve to be happy." Michael raised up in bed. "Payton, you think Liz will stay? I don't know what I'd do if she left and took the boys. It would be my fault." Tears rolled down Michael's cheeks, and all Sin could do was hold him and pray.

Summer got cans of soda from the vending machine, then they found an empty bench in the inner courtyard of the hospital with a water fountain and clay pots spilling over with colorful impatiens and dragon-wing begonia. The setting should have been peaceful, but Summer could feel the tension and anger simmering from the other woman.

"I've always been a good listener." Summer placed her handbag next to her and casually sipped her drink. "And I won't betray a confidence."

"Don't be the fool I was." Liz's hand clenched the soda can. "I believed Michael, put it out of my mind."

"You feel he betrayed you by becoming ill," Summer said.

"He did," she answered tightly. "I trusted him, loved him, and he lied to me."

"If he's anything like Sin, Michael loves his family. More than you, he has to be aware that he let you down," Summer reasoned. "It can't be easy for him."

"It's his fault that our boys are in danger, that he . . ." Liz put her hand over her mouth.

Summer blinked back her own tears, placed the can on the small patch of slate by her feet, and caught Liz's free hand. "I won't insult you by saying I know how you must feel. I can't imagine a worse hell than fearing for the man I love and our children, unless it was going through it alone."

"I want to leave, run away," Liz whispered. "Just take the boys and go."

"I can't tell you what to do. You have to do what you feel is best for everyone concerned."

"You wouldn't," Liz commented—a statement, not a question.

"I'd like to think not." She squeezed Liz's hand. "I lost both of my parents when I was eighteen. Sin helped me though those difficult days and weeks. I know what it is to live with regrets, to cherish the memories. At the moment Sin is all right. He refuses to be tested, and I have to honor his decision. But I won't give him up, I won't throw away the time we have. He's fighting me, but I intend to win on this."

"You love him that much?" Liz asked.

"I love him that much."

Liz pulled her hand away. "I'd like to sit here by myself."

"Of course." Summer picked up her can and handbag and rose to her feet. Liz's shoulders were hunched over, her hands clasped tightly together in her lap. It was anybody's guess if she would run or stay.

Liz had been gone more than an hour. Michael kept looking at the clock in his room, his expression more fearful as the minutes ticked by. Sin couldn't take it any longer. "I need a soft drink. You want one?"

"No." Michael never lifted his head from the pillow or looked at Sin.

"Be back in a couple of minutes." Sin pushed open the door and went down the hall toward the waiting room. Passing the short hall for the elevators, he saw Summer sitting on a bench in front of the window. She put away her phone and came to her feet.

"Where's Liz?"

"I left her downstairs. She wanted to sit by herself," Summer told him.

Sin briefly closed his eyes, then pulled Summer back down the hallway toward Michael's room. He'd hoped Liz was stronger than this. "Is she thinking of not coming back?"

Summer caught his hand. Misery stared back at him. "I'm sorry."

"He was afraid of this." Sin frowned. "Is that why you were sitting out there alone?"

"I didn't want either of you to see me without her. Every time the elevator doors opened, I hoped it was her."

"This is going to kill him." Sin took her arms. "I'd rather you walk away now than later."

"I'm staying."

"So am I." Liz stood a few feet away. "I thought about what you said, Summer. Despite everything, I love Michael. It won't be easy, but I won't leave him when he needs me the most."

"He loves you, too, Liz," Sin said.

"I think I'd like to hear him tell me that." Liz continued down the hall and into her husband's room.

Sin opened the door, saw his brother and wife embracing, and quietly let it swing shut. "Let's go grab a bite, and give them a few minutes."

Sin took Summer's bag from his driver, caught her arm, and went up the bricked steps to his house. It was past midnight. The nurses had finally run them all out. Shortly after seven, the twins had come with videos of their football practice. They'd watched it together, with Michael critiquing while Liz sat on his bed.

Sin was realistic enough to accept that there would be difficult days ahead, but they were going through them together as a family. Counseling would help, but so would love. Michael and Liz had decided to wait until the boys were eighteen to discuss their father's illness, and at that time they could decide if they wanted to be tested. No one felt it would be fair to tell the twins now.

"I'll show you to your room."

"Is it where you're sleeping?"

"I thought we put our relationship on hold."

"I lied." She went to him. "I love you. Seeing what Liz and Michael are going though, I ached for them, but I don't plan to waste time."

"Summer—"

"No. We're better together than we are apart." She took the case from his hand. "Which way?"

"It doesn't matter what I say."

"Only one thing."

"What's that?"

"That you love me. I'd like to hear you say the words."

He went to her. "I don't know when or how it happened, I'm only grateful that it did." He palmed her face. "I love you. You make the hell I'm going though bearable."

The case hit the floor. "Sin, I love you so much. I was so afraid I'd never hear you say you loved me."

"I do love you, I'm just beginning to realize how much. It's selfish of me to want to keep you, but I don't think I could make it without you in my life."

"While I was waiting at the elevator, I used my phone to do a search on the Internet on Huntington's. It made me love you more. I want this time with you. I want to cherish each day and not waste it."

"But your life is in New York."

"My life is with you. And who says I can't have two restaurants if I decide one day? You have six offices."

"I can't have children," he reminded her.

"Then we can adopt or mentor. There are kids that need us and we'll find them. We'll make a great aunt and uncle to Jadon and Jardon. As long as we have each other, we can do anything."

He stared into her eyes, closed his briefly. "Last chance to get out of here. I'm not having the genetic testing done."

"Your decision. I love you. We'll face tomorrow together."

He swallowed. "I love you. I don't want to live without you."

"You don't have to. Now all we have to do is

figure out if we want a quiet wedding now or a big one later on."

"Marriage?" He was a bit stunned.

She kissed him. "I want it all, and I want it all with you."

He realized he did as well. She made him courageous enough to fight for their happiness, their love. "So do I. I want the whole world to know you belong to me." His arms pulled her tighter. "Whatever else happens in my life, I'm thankful I have you."

"We have each other. Now take me to bed."

"Gladly." He picked her up. "We can leave the case. You won't need the nightgown you brought."

She nipped his ear. "I didn't bring one."

Laughing, he continued to his bedroom with his woman, his world.

Epilogue

Evelyn Callahan was in her element as she prepared another celebratory engagement brunch. She couldn't believe Sin and Summer were engaged. She hadn't had a clue they were any more than friends.

A pleased smile on her face, she paused in fussing over the flower arrangement on the table on the terrace, swallowed, thought of her sister, Summer's mother, Caroline. She would have been so happy for this day and so proud of her daughter. Terrance, her husband, would have taken Sin aside and had a quiet talk with him. Last night when Sin and Summer had arrived back from Dallas, Evelyn's husband had spoken quietly with Sin and welcomed him into the family.

Leaving the roses, Evelyn walked to the end of the terrace and stared out at the calm blue water. Her hand shielding her eyes, she saw the *Wind Catcher* riding the waves. Sin had rented the small yacht to take his and Summer's guests sailing. The day was picture-perfect. Sin's brother and his family along with C. J., Cicely, Alex, Dianne, Evelyn's husband, their daughter Ariel, and their son Paul and his wife and children, were on the yacht, but Sin and Summer were somewhere walking on the beach.

Evelyn looked down the beach searching for Sin and Summer, then glanced at her watch. Everyone should be back in less than fifteen minutes. She headed to the kitchen. She wanted everything to be perfect for her other daughter and the man she loved.

Arm in arm Sin and Summer strolled along the beach. Earlier they had waved to their guests as the *Wind Catcher* headed out to sea for a short run. Deep in thought, his head down, Sin was nervous and tried to think of the right words.

"If you're thinking of running, I'll hunt you down and do horrible things to your body," Summer said, her voice light and teasing.

Stopping, his head came up. He stared into her beautiful eyes, but more than that saw her beautiful heart. His hands came up to frame her precious face. His turbulent thoughts settled when he remembered the words she'd told him in the hospital. *Just say what's in your heart.* "I love you."

Her hands covered his. "And I love you right back."

His forehead rested against hers for a second before he straightened. "I had the genetic testing done. It's negative."

She gasped. Her eyes widened as her arms went

around him, holding him tightly. Tears dampened his shirt.

He held her just as tightly. "I didn't feel it fair for you to marry me and not know. I could have lived with knowing I had the disease, but I couldn't bear you not honestly knowing what you might have to go through."

Her head lifted. Tears shimmered in her eyes. "You are the most courageous and loving man I know."

His thumb brushed the moisture away from her cheeks. "I can't pass on the disease since I don't have the defective gene, but I still don't want to consider having the vasectomy reversed."

"I told you in Dallas, there are children we can mentor or adopt if we decide to later." She brushed her lips across his. "I have you and that's more than I ever imagined. We'll take it as it comes. I can't wait until our wedding day."

"Then I guess I better give you this." He drew a ring out of his pocket and slid it on the third finger of her unsteady left hand. "I love you, Summer. You're the one and only."

Summer stared down at the large round purplish pink diamond surrounded by flawless white diamonds. The stones sparkled and glittered in the bright sunlight. Her heart pounded.

"Say something. Don't you like it? Liz helped. I wanted a stone as rare and as precious as you are. I was sure—"

Her mouth on his stopped his panicky flow of words. "It's absolutely perfect. Just like you. Just like our love."

"A loved that saved me." He kissed her, drew her securely into his arms.

Life didn't offer any guarantees, but he was holding one in his arms. Whatever happened, this courageous and loving woman would be beside him. He caught her hand wearing his ring and started back up the beach with an unshakable certainty that no matter what lay ahead, they had each other.

It was enough.

ALSO BY FRANCIS RAY

THE GRAYSONS SERIES

Until There Was You
Only You
Irresistible You
Dreaming of You
You and No Other

GRAYSON FRIENDS SERIES

With Just One Kiss
A Seductive Kiss
It Had to Be You
One Night With You
Nobody But You
The Way You Love Me

. . . and look for

I KNOW WHO HOLDS TOMORROW

Coming in November 2012

Available from St. Martin's Paperbacks